SNOWBOUND

"Mum, are you positive you know how to get home from here? I mean are you absolutely positive?"

Mum gave me a look. "Stacey, we're not lost," she said.

"Well, do you know where we are?" . . .

"Darling, if I didn't know where we were then I wouldn't know where to go. Relax, okay?" . . .

Mum rocked the car a few times, then rushed around and tried to drive us out of the snowy rut our wheels had created. It was no use.

We were stuck.

We were stranded!

When it finally starts to snow in Stoneybrook, it doesn't stop, and nobody's prepared for it. Mallory and Mary Anne are snowed in with the Pike kids, Jessi's stranded at her dance school, and Claudia's alone with the Perkins Girls. But what about Stacey and her mum? They've been gone for *hours* in the car. Where on earth can they be?

SNOWBOUND

Ann M. Martin

Hippo Books
Scholastic Children's Books
London

*This special book is for
a very special person,
Nikki Vach.*

Scholastic Children's Books,
Scholastic Publications Ltd,
7–9 Pratt Street, London NW1 0AE, UK

Scholastic Inc.,
730 Broadway, New York, NY 10003, USA

Scholastic Canada Ltd,
123 Newkirk Road, Richmond Hill,
Ontario, Canada L4C 3G5

Ashton Scholastic Pty Ltd,
P O Box 579, Gosford, New South Wales,
Australia

Ashton Scholastic Ltd,
Private Bag 1, Penrose, Auckland,
New Zealand

First published in the US by Scholastic Inc., 1991
First published in the UK by Scholastic Publications Ltd, 1992

Copyright © Ann M Martin, 1991

ISBN 0 590 55110 8

Typeset in Plantin by Contour Typesetters, Southall, London
Printed by Cox & Wyman Ltd, Reading, Berks

10 9 8 7 6 5 4 3 2 1

Ms. Kristy Thomas
1210 McLelland Road
Stoneybrook, CT 06800

Ms. Marian Tan, Editor
The Stoneybrook News
One Stoneybrook Plaza
Stoneybrook, CT 06800

Dear Mrs. Tan:

Hi! My name is Kristy Thomas. (Well, I suppose you already knew that from the return address.) I am thirteen years old and I'm an eighth-grader at Stoneybrook Middle School. I am writing you to find out if you're interested in an article on that blizzard we had last week. The article you published in your newspaper after the storm was very informative, but it didn't tell what happened to people during the blizzard. My friends and I had lots of adventures and different experiences. One of my friends even got stranded in a car and almost froze to death! Some funny things happened, too. My friends and I are very close, and we share our lives with each other. So after the blizzard, we each wrote down

how we weathered the storm. Get it?
WEATHERed the STORM? Anyway, then we
passed our stories around so we
could read them. The stories are
fascinating (really—— I'm not bragging),
so I thought other people might want
to read them, too.

If you would like to print a young
people's account of the blizzard, just
let me know. I will be happy to edit
my friends' stories and make them
into an article. It can be however
long you want.

I won't hold any rights to the story,
but I would appreciate it if you
would print "By Kristy Thomas" under
the big headline that reads "SNOWBOUND!"

Yours sincerely,
Kristy Thomas

P.S. If you want to pay me, I
   wouldn't mind. How much do
   reporters earn? (I won't be
   too picky.)
P.P.S. Do you have any children? If
    so, I know a good baby-
    sitting ser

2

"Kristy rub that out!"

"What?"

"Rub out that P.P.S. This is a letter about a newspaper article, not the Babysitters Club."

My best friend, Mary Anne Spier, is far too practical. I didn't think an announcement about our business could hurt anything. Even so, I took out the P.P.S. It wasn't worth arguing over.

You'll never believe what happened to me and my friends in the Babysitters Club (BSC) when a huge blizzard hit our little town of Stoneybrook, Connecticut, last week. The storm caught everyone by surprise, and different things happened to all of us. Some of our adventures were scary, some were exciting . . . and mine was funny! Most of us were separated during the storm. We couldn't contact each other either, because after a while, the phone lines went down. (Also, the power went out.) So we didn't hear about the adventures until the next day, when we could gossip on the phone again.

Considering how fascinating our experiences were, I was surprised to read the article headed "Blizzard" in the paper the next day. I know I told the editor, Marian Tan, that the article was very informative (and it was), but the truth is, it was also incredibly boring. It mentioned lots of facts and statistics. For instance, about 70cm of snow fell in Stoneybrook, and there was a wind chill factor of minus 8 degrees. But the article didn't say anything about *people*. There was no human interest. What about the cars that got stranded (I mean, with people in them)? What about parents who had left their children with babysitters and couldn't get home to them? And what about people who got stuck at airports?

I decided that my article would give people the kind of news they wanted. Interesting news. If only Marian Tan would print it.

"Mary Anne?" I said. "How long do you think we'll have to wait to hear from the editor?" (I'm not the most patient person in the world.)

"I don't know," she answered. "In the meantime, let's go over the material you've collected."

1st CHAPTER

Kristy

Sunday

Sunday was a pretty normal weekend day. Homework. Spending time with my family. Talking to Bart on the phone. Even the weather report was normal (but boring). The newscaster was predicting a snowstorm. Big deal. It was the fourth storm that had been predicted in two weeks and not a single flake of snow had fallen. I turned off the radio and went back to my homework. Here's how boring the snowstorm prediction was: My homework seemed fascinating in comparison....

"Kristy, please can you help me with my jumper?"

I turned round. I was sitting at the desk in my room, slaving over a maths problem. Since I was nowhere near solving it, I didn't mind the interruption. My stepsister, Karen, was standing in the doorway.

"For heaven's sake! Why are you wearing your jumper on your legs?" I asked. Karen had put her legs through her jumper sleeves and was now struggling to hold the bottom of the jumper round her waist.

"It's a new style," Karen replied. "Jumper pants." She hobbled over to my desk. "Can you button me up at the back, please?"

"I've got a feeling," I said as I fastened the button, "that this isn't what Nannie had in mind when she knitted this jumper for you."

Nannie's my grandmother. She and Karen are just two of the people in my big, jumbly family. The others are my mum; my stepfather, Watson; my three brothers (Charlie, who's seventeen; Sam, who's fifteen; and David Michael, who's seven); my stepbrother, Andrew (he's four and Karen's seven); and my adopted sister, Emily Michelle. Emily's two and a half. Mum and Watson adopted her from Vietnam. I don't really think of her as my *adopted* sister. She's just my sister, the same as Karen and Andrew are just my sister and brother.

That's a big family, isn't it? Nannie's Mum's mother. She helps look after Emily while Mum and Watson are at work. Karen and Andrew are Watson's children from his first marriage. Usually, they live with us every other weekend, but this December they were living with us for two weeks while their mum and stepfather went on a skiing holiday. (Karen and Andrew's other house is right here in Stoneybrook, not far from their father's house.) They had arrived yesterday. When Karen's here, things are never dull.

Karen pranced out of my room, wearing her jumper-pants.

"What are you going to do now?" I asked her.

"Play with Emily Junior." (Emily is Karen's rat. Karen named her after Emily Michelle. I think that was a compliment.)

I turned back to my homework, but those numbers and signs seemed to swim around on the paper. I let my mind wander. It wandered right to the Winter Wonderland Dance. It was going to be held on Friday evening after school, and it would be quite a big do. It was for every pupil at SMS—sixth-graders, seventh-graders, and eighth-graders. For once, every single one of my friends and I had a partner for the dance. We'd planned to go together, seven girls and seven boys. We couldn't wait. The decorating committee was going to transform the SMS gym into a snowy fairyland—sparkly flakes and white cotton-drifts, tinsel icicles. It would be wonderful.

In the past, I haven't given much thought to dances, but now they're a little more important to me. That's because I've got a friend. I mean, a friend who's a boy. Oh, all right. He's my boyfriend. I suppose. I never thought I'd have a boyfriend. My friends say I'm a tomboy, and I suppose that's true. I love sport. I'm happiest wearing jeans and trainers. Basically, I think make-up's a waste of time. And jewellery? I can take it or leave it. I haven't even got pierced ears.

But then I met Bart.

Now everything's different. No, that's not true. Bart and I met because we each coach a softball team for little kids. So our friendship is founded on sport. I'd still rather wear jeans than a dress, and I'm not planning to get my ears pierced. But . . . I look forward to spending time with Bart. And I was particularly looking foward to going to the Winter Wonderland Dance with him. I was even looking forward to wearing a dress (since I'd only be in it for a few hours). Besides, going to a dance with all my friends and all their partners would be really fun. Mary Anne and I had been talking about the dance for weeks. We were going to buy carnations for the boys. (We had a feeling they might be buying corsages for us.)

I could hear the phone ring then. It brought me

back to reality, and I tried to concentrate on the maths problem.

"Kris-teeee!" I heard David Michael call from the first floor. "Phone for you! It's your *boyfriend*. It's . . . *Bart, Bart bo Bart, banana fana fo—*"

I was at the top of the stairs before David Michael could sing another syllable of his stupid song. "Be *quiet*!" I hissed. "Do you want Bart to hear you?"

"Yes," replied David Michael. He started the song all over again.

I sprinted into Mum's room, grabbed the receiver off the phone, and began talking loudly, hoping Bart wouldn't hear my brother. At last David Michael whispered, "Cowabunga, dude!" into the phone, and then (thankfully) put down the extension.

"Sorry about that," I said to Bart.

"Who wound him up?" was Bart's reply.

"Oh, no one. It's Christmas, I think. Karen's loony, too."

"Actually, so's my little brother. But he's loony because he *still* thinks we're going to get some snow."

I laughed. "The only snowflakes we're going to see will be decorating the walls of the gym for the dance on Friday. Oh, by the way," I went on, trying to sound nonchalant, "what colour suit are you wearing?"

"Puce."

Puce? Where was I going to find a puce carnation? Even worse, my dress was red. We were going to clash horribly. That's the problem with dressing up. You have to worry about things like colours clashing. Or whether your petticoat's showing. "Puce?" I repeated.

"Well, not really. I'm just teasing, Kristy. My suit's black."

That made life easier. Almost any colour goes with black. Even grey. I almost giggled. I pictured myself in the flower shop, asking the assistant for a grey carnation. "It's for an elephant," I would tell him.

Bart and I spoke for a few more minutes. We rang off when I heard Karen screaming from the playroom. I ran to her. "For heaven's sake, what's the matter?"

"Emily Junior's gone!" wailed Karen.

Sure enough, the rat cage was empty. Great! Mum and Nannie were going to love this.

Watson wouldn't be too pleased either, for that matter.

"What happened?" I asked. (I could hear the rest of my family making a dash for the playroom.)

"She's just gone," replied Karen. "Kidnapped, probably." (Karen's got mysteries and detective stories on the brain.) "No sign of a struggle, though."

Guess what? My family searched high and low for Emily Junior that evening—and we couldn't

10

find her. Oh, goody! A rat was missing in our house. Now I could relax!

I went back to my room and the maths problem. After I'd stared at my paper for ages and still couldn't work out what to do next, I stood up, stretched, and switched on my stereo. I tuned the radio to WSTO, the Voice of Stoneybrook. Can you believe it? The weatherwoman (that's what *I* call her, even though the people on WSTO call her a weather*girl*) was predicting snow again. She said the storm would hit us the next day.

What a laugh!

I turned off the radio. I finished my homework. Then I read a story to Andrew and David Michael. Andrew, thinking positively, had requested that I read *Katy and the Big Snow*. So I did. Then I helped him get ready for bed. I was all ready to *put* him to bed, too, but he asked for Daddy, so I called Watson upstairs.

Then I checked Karen. She was crawling around on her hands and knees. I knew she was looking for Emily Junior again.

"Karen," I said, "I'm sure she'll turn up."

Karen got to her feet. "I suppose," she replied.

"It's supposed to snow tomorrow," I told her, trying to cheer her up.

Karen transformed before my eyes. "*Is* it?" (She never gets tired of hoping for snow.)

"Oh, yippee, yippee, yippeeeee!" she screeched.

I went back to my room, opened my wardrobe,

and gazed for a while at the red dress for the Winter Wonderland Dance.

That night, I dreamed of snowflakes and carnations and Bart. In the dream, a storm hit Stoneybrook. Only it snowed fat white carnations, which showered down on Bart and me.

2nd CHAPTER

Claudia

Heres how to descibe monday. *monday* Partly claudy and cold but not to cold. So where was our snow. Once again it didnt' arrive. This afternon I baby sat for Myria and Gabie and Laura perkins. Mariah and Gabby were realy disapperntened about the snow. I mean the no snow. They have been waiting patently for a storm or even a flury.

OK, I know I'm not a very good speller. So what?

Oops! Sorry. I know I sound defensive. My friend Stacey McGill tells me I do. Kristy does, too, of course. If something's on her mind, she says it.

I'm Claudia Kishi. I'm one of the members of the Babysitters Club. In fact, I'm the vice-chairman. And I'm *not* a good speller, or even a very good pupil, but my friends don't care. (I wish my parents and teachers would follow their example!)

Well, another snowy forecast, another wrong prediction. There was only one good thing about the lack of snow. I didn't have to worry about whether the SMS Winter Wonderland Dance would be held. In past years, it's been cancelled three times due to bad weather. And I wanted desperately to go. My escort was going to be Iri Mitsuhashi, this boy who's in a couple of my classes. We aren't girlfriend-and-boyfriend or anything, but we're friends and we have fun together. In case you're wondering, Iri is Japanese. So am I. Well, we're Japanese-American. Our parents were born in Japan; we were born in America.

Here are the reasons why I wanted snow:

I wanted school to be cancelled. (I usually do.)

I wanted snow for Christmas.

The kids in Stoneybrook were going crazy because practically every other day, snow was forecast—and then it didn't come. That Monday afternoon, the Perkins girls were pretty disappointed. And they weren't the only ones.

"The triplets are driving me mad!" exploded Mallory Pike as she came into my room for that day's BSC meeting. "All they do is complain because they haven't been able to build a snowman yet."

"Tell me about it!" replied Jessi Ramsey. "Becca's been moping for days."

"Well, guess what I did?" said Kristy. "Last night I told Karen we were supposed to have snow today. I told her because she was upset that Emily Junior's missing—"

"*Is* she?" interrupted Mary Anne. "Remind me not to babysit at your house till . . . till the problem's been sorted out."

"So now," Kristy continued, "Emily's still missing *and* it hasn't snowed."

The time was 5:23, according to my digital clock (the official club timekeeper). Three afternoons a week—Mondays, Wednesdays, and Fridays, from five-thirty till six—the members of the BSC hold a meeting. The members are Kristy Thomas, me, Stacey McGill, Mary Anne Spier, Dawn Schafer, Mallory Pike, and Jessi Ramsey. What do we do at our meetings? We take phonecalls from people in Stoneybrook who need babysitters for their children. My friends and I get lots of jobs that way. Our club has become a real business. And we run it professionally.

Kristy's the chairman. The club was her idea. She worked out how to run it efficiently, and she keeps the rest of us on our toes!

I'm the vice-chairman because the meetings are held in my room. They're held there because I'm the only one of us who's got a private phone and a private phone number. This is important. We get a lot of calls during most of our meetings, and we'd hate to tie up some grown-up's phone three times a week.

Stacey McGill is our treasurer. She collects weekly subs and keeps track of the money we earn. She's also my best friend—the first best friend I've ever had. Stacey and I are alike in that we both adore wild clothes and wild jewellery, doing our hair, painting our nails—that sort of thing. (I even have two holes pierced in one ear, and one hole in the other. Stacey just has one hole in each ear.) Sometimes, since I *love* art, I make jewellery for us. To be honest, I must add that Stacey and I (and this isn't bragging) are a little more sophisticated than the other club members —even Dawn, Mary Anne, and Kristy, who are thirteen-year-old SMS eighth-graders, just like Stacey and me. (Jessi and Mal are eleven and in the sixth grade at SMS).Stacey and I have really different lives, though. Stacey's parents are divorced, and she's an only child. My parents aren't divorced, and I've got an older sister,

Janine. Stacey grew up in New York. I grew up here in Stoneybrook. (Stacey still visits New York regularly, though, because her dad lives there.) One other difference: Stacey's got a disease called diabetes. I don't understand the technical stuff about her illness, but I do know that she has to be very careful about what she eats because her body doesn't break down blood sugar properly. Too much or too little sugar and she can get *really* ill. (Stacey's got a severe form of the disease. She's called a brittle diabetic.) Every day, she has to test her blood, count calories, pay strict attention to her diet (no sweets or sticky pudding, which would be a real trial for me, since I'm a junk-food addict), and give herself injections of this stuff called insulin. (The idea of giving myself a jab makes me feel sick, but not Stacey. She's used to it.)

The club secretary is Mary Anne Spier. Her job is to organize the BSC record book—keep it up-to-date and accurate. To do that, Mary Anne has to know the complicated schedules of the seven club members. Then, when someone calls needing a babysitter, Mary Anne can check the appointment pages in the book and see who's free to take the job. Being the secretary isn't easy, but Mary Anne's a very careful worker.

Mary Anne is Kristy's best friend, but she's really different from her. She's shy, she's soft-spoken, she cries easily—and she's got a steady boyfriend! His name is Logan Bruno. (Of course,

Logan and Mary Anne were going to go to the Winter Wonderland Dance together.) Mary Anne grew up with just her dad. She had no brothers and sisters, and her mum died when Mary Anne was a baby. But things have changed. Mr Spier recently remarried. And guess who his new wife is? Dawn Schafer's mother. So now Mary Anne and Dawn are stepsisters *and* best friends. (Mary Anne's lucky. She's got two best friends.) Mary Anne, Dawn, and their dad and mum live in a wonderful old farmhouse that Mrs Schafer bought.

Dawn is the alternate officer of the BSC. This means she can fill in for any other officer if that person has to miss a meeting for some reason. Dawn has to know everything—how to schedule appointments, how to keep track of the money in the treasury, etc. Her job isn't easy, but since club members rarely miss meetings, she doesn't have to take over very often.

You might be wondering how Dawn's mum and Mary Anne's dad got together. This is an interesting story. Both Mr Spier and Mrs Schafer grew up in Stoneybrook. They went out together in high school, but they lost track of each other when Mrs Schafer left for college in California. While she was on the West Coast, she met Mr Schafer and got married, and they had Dawn and Dawn's younger brother, Jeff. When Dawn was twelve, though, her parents decided to get divorced, so Mrs Schafer moved back to Stoneybrook with Dawn and Jeff. She met Mr Spier again (who was Mary Anne's father by then) and they got married the following year. That's when Mary Anne and Dawn became stepsisters. Now the Spiers and Schafers are one big happy family—most of the time. They've had their share of problems. I suppose the worst was that Jeff never grew to like Stoneybrook. He just wasn't happy here. So he went back to California to live with his dad. Dawn and Jeff see each other pretty often, though. They fly across the country a lot, and they run up *huge* phone bills!

Our California girl is beautiful. Her hair's long and shiny and so blonde it's practically white. Her eyes are blue and she looks . . . healthy. I'm not sure how to describe that. Glowing, maybe? Anyway, this might be a result of the tons of health food Dawn eats. She's as addicted to raw vegetables and tofu as I am to Hula Hoops and crisps. We could never live together, but I think Stacey enjoys having Dawn around because the two of them can turn down my goodies and stuff themselves with whatever appeals to them— pretzels, crackers, things without sugar. Yuck. I love Dawn in spite of this, though. She's an individual, sure of herself (mostly), happy to go her own way, dress her own way, make her own friends. Everyone's glad Dawn came to Connecticut and joined the club.

Jessi Ramsey and Mal Pike (their names are shortened versions of Jessica and Mallory) are the BSC's junior officers. They haven't got actual club duties. "Junior officer" means that since they're younger than the rest of us, they aren't allowed to babysit at night, unless they're taking care of their own brothers and sisters. They're a big help, anyway. Since they take over a lot of the afternoon and weekend jobs, they free us older sitters for the evenings.

Like Stacey and me, Mal and Jessi are best friends. Their lives are similar in many ways. They're both the oldest child in the family; they feel that, despite this, their parents still treat them like babies; and they love reading, especially horse stories and mysteries. There are some differences, too, of course. While Jessi has one younger sister and a baby brother, Mal has *seven* younger sisters and brothers. Three of them are ten-year-old identical triplets (Byron, Jordan, and Adam). Then there's Vanessa, Nicky, Margo, and Claire. Claire's the baby. Well, she's five, but she's the youngest in the family. Mal and Jessi may love reading, but Jessi's real interest is ballet, and Mal's is writing. You should see Jessi dance! (I have.) She's incredible. She goes to classes at a special dance school in Stamford, a city not far from Stoneybrook. She had to audition just to be able to go there. And she's danced the leading role in several productions, performing on stage in front of hundreds of people. Mal, on the other hand, hopes to be an author one day. She likes to draw too, so she thinks she might become a children's author and illustrator. Guess what? Even though they're only eleven, Mal and Jessi both have semi-boyfriends who are taking them to the Winter Wonderland Dance. Mal's is Ben Hobart. He's new at SMS and he's Australian! (He and his family live opposite me, next door to the Perkinses.) Jessi's is Quint Walter. She met him in New York, which is where he lives. Quint's a ballet dancer too, and goes to a special performing arts school. Jessi and Quint haven't seen each other since Jessi's trip to the city—but in just two days, Quint will be travelling to Stoneybrook to stay with the Ramseys and go to the dance. As you can imagine, Mal and Jessi are nearly hysterical with excitement over the dance. Let me see. Oh, yes. One other thing—Mal's white and Jessi's black.

"Listen, everyone, we've got a lot to talk about . . . Are you listening?"

That was Kristy. She had called the club meeting to order about six times, and the rest of us were still jabbering away.

"Hey, I was thinking!" shouted Kristy. "We might as well cancel our next meeting. So many of us are going to be busy on Wednesday." That got our attention. Club meetings are rarely cancelled.

21

"Mal and I will be babysitting," said Mary Anne. "That's the marathon when Mr and Mrs Pike go to New York for a day and won't be home till about one in the morning or something. I'm spending the night at Mal's." (The Pikes have got so many children that they need *two* babysitters.) "Who else is busy?"

"I am," replied Jessi. "Rehearsal for *The Nutcracker*."

"I might be, remember?" added Dawn. "Jeff's coming home for Christmas some time that evening. I'm not sure when Mum and I will be leaving to pick him up at the airport."

"I'm babysitting for the Perkins girls again on Wednesday evening," I said, "but I'll be around in the afternoon. Why don't I stay here and take phone messages? I don't mind."

We decided that was a good idea. Then we spent the rest of the meeting answering job calls, scheduling appointments, and talking about the dance. I have to admit that the dance was a pretty big do. For instance, Kristy had invited Bart, who doesn't go to our school, and Jessi was going to introduce Quint to the other pupils at SMS. An out-of-town boyfriend was quite special. Besides, I don't know about anyone else, but *I* was really looking forward to dressing up. I'd bought this black velvet knickerbocker outfit and was going to wear it with a lot of silver jewellery, including snowflake earrings. Now, if only the weather would cool off and it would snow for real!

3rd CHAPTER

Dawn

Monday

I was sorry we had to cancel a club meeting, that's for sure, but I couldn't wait to see Jeff on Wednesday. It seemed as if years had passed since we were last together. (Actually, it was only a few weeks.) I wouldn't even mind the boring car ride to the airport, since when we got there, Mum and I would soon be reunited with Jeff. Mary Anne, I wish you could have come with us, but you were on your babysitting marathon. Oh, well. You would see Jeff Thursday morning.

Dawn

"Goodbye!"

" 'Bye, everyone!"

"See you tomorrow!"

"Don't forget—no Wednesday meeting!"

Our Monday BSC meeting was breaking up. It was Claud who'd reminded us that the next meeting had been cancelled.

And it was Mary Anne who said, "Wait a sec! The dance!"

"What about it?" I asked.

"The dance is on Friday evening. If we skip our Wednesday meeting, the next meeting should be on Friday, but can we hold a meeting right before the dance?"

"Well, we'd better not cancel two meetings in a row," said Kristy. "Don't worry. We'll work something out. See you all in school tomorrow!"

We weren't worried. We were too excited to be worried. So much was going on. Jeff was arriving, Mary Anne's big Pike job was coming up, Christmas was approaching, and then there was the dance, of course. I was going to go with Price Irving, this boy at school. He wasn't new or anything, but I hadn't noticed him until a few weeks ago. Overnight, I'd developed an amazing crush on him. And then he'd invited me to go to the dance with him. The weird thing is that I'd just plucked up courage to invite *him*, and the very next day I was dashing along the corridors at school, trying to get from one class to another

24

without killing myself as I dodged through the crowd, when I ran slap bang into Price.

I almost said, "Oh, my lord!" which is what Claudia would have said, but I stopped myself in time and simply said, "Sorry." (Meanwhile, this little voice in my brain was chanting, "You're such a jerk! You're such a jerk!") How could I ask him out *now*?

Price solved the problem for me. He grinned. "That's okay," he replied. "I'm glad you ran into me." (I laughed.) "I wanted to ask you something. Um, Dawn, um, Dawn, um—"

"Yes?" I prompted him.

After about half an hour (well, not really), Price managed to invite me to the dance. Of course I accepted. I'm no fool. And now the dance was just four days away, and I'd bought a new dress and everything.

Life was good.

"Excited, darling?" Mum asked me after supper that night.

"Very. It's going to be dreamy," I said, and sighed.

Mum frowned. "Dreamy?"

"Yes. He's so . . . incredible."

"Incredible? Jeff?"

"No, Price," I said.

Mum laughed. "I meant, are you excited about Jeff's visit?"

25

"Oh! I thought you were asking about the dance. Yes. Of course I'm excited. I can't wait to see Jeff. Dad, too."

My winter holiday was going to be busy. Jeff would stay with us until the day after Christmas, and then he and I were going to fly back to California and I would stay with Dad and Jeff until New Year's Day.

"Can I ring Jeff?" I asked Mum. I looked at my watch. "It's five o'clock out there. This is probably a good time to reach him."

"Of course dear," said Mum. "Go ahead. Ask him about his flight while you're at it."

I dialled California. The phone rang twice before someone picked it up. "Simpson's Clothing Boutique. Bra department," said a voice.

"Jeff!" I exclaimed.

"Uh-oh. Dawn?"

"Yes."

"I thought you were going to be Oliver."

I giggled. "Anyway, hi! Can you talk for a minute? Mum said I could phone you. Is this a good time?"

"Fine."

"I'm sorry I'm not Oliver. I just wanted to ask you about Wednesday. You're still on the same flight?"

"Yup." Jeff paused. "It stops in Chicago, though."

"I know. But it just stops, right? You don't

have to change planes or anything, do you?" Not that it would matter. Jeff's a champion flyer.

"Nope. Just a stop."

"Have you got enough to do on the plane?"

"Yup."

"Jeff, is anything wrong?" My brother may not be a big talker, but he can usually do better than this.

"Well, I was thinking. What if we were flying along and suddenly the plane lost its engine power and we crashed? What if we flew right into a mountain like those people did in that film?"

"That isn't going to happen," I said.

"How do you know?"

"I don't . . . But we've both flown lots of times, and the worst flight we ever had was that really, really bumpy one."

"Yes. You never know, though."

My stomach began to feel funny. "Jeff, you are coming, aren't you?" I asked.

"I wish I didn't have to fly," was his answer.

"Oh, Jeff, please! It's Christmas. We're waiting till you come before we decorate the tree. Don't stay in California. You've got to come." Even as the words were leaving my mouth, I knew I'd said the wrong thing.

"I don't *have* to come," replied Jeff.

"No. No, you don't. I didn't mean that. I'm just looking forward to your visit."

"But what if the plane *does* crash?"

"What if it doesn't and you stay in California and miss a wonderful trip to see Mum and me?"

"At least I'll be alive."

I sighed.

When Jeff and I rang off, I told Mum about our conversation.

Mum frowned slightly, but she said, "Don't worry. Jeff will be all right. I think he's just going through a phase." (This is a very parent thing to say. According to adults, children are always going through phases.) "Jeff's reacting to the divorce," Mum went on. "He's having a little trouble with separation. He'll be okay once he gets here."

I nodded. "In two days the flight will be over. Then Jeff can relax." So could I. I'd feel better when he was actually in our house.

While Mary Anne and I were getting ready for bed that night, we tuned into WTSO, our local radio station. "Hey, listen!" said Mary Anne, putting down her hairbrush.

"Snow is on the way!" the weather forecaster was saying. "Heavy falls expected on Wednesday."

"Yes, okay," I said, and shook my head.

4th CHAPTER

Mallory

Tuesday

Yes! Mum and Dad were going to leave for New York EARLY the next morning. Then Mary Anne and I would be in charge for almost 24 hours! Mary Anne was going to spend TWO nights at my house, starting that night. (That was so she wouldn't have to come over at the crack of dawn in the morning, when my parents left for the train.) It was going to be one of the biggest, most important babysitting jobs ever. Mum and Dad wouldn't be back until after MIDNIGHT!

29

When Mum and Dad first started talking about this trip to New York, a tiny part of me hoped I might be left in charge (well, accompanied by another babysitter, since that's the Pike rule). Then I found out that my parents were going to leave extra early in the morning and wouldn't be back until about 2 am.

I lost all hope.

But *then* Mum and Dad said that if an older sitter (thirteen's *so* much older than eleven) would spend Tuesday and Wednesday nights at our house, they would consider letting me take on half the job. (The holiday spirit must have been getting the better of them.) As it turned out, Mary Anne was able to do the job with me. I couldn't believe her father would allow her to sleep at someone's house for two nights in a row during school. But he did. (The holiday spirit must have been getting to him, too. Our parents were acting so . . . sane.)

"So what are you going to do on your trip to the Big Apple?" I asked Mum one day. I myself have been to New York several times.

"Lots of things," Mum replied. "Your dad and I have planned quite a day. We're going to eat a light breakfast at the Embassy—"

"That *coffee* shop?" I exclaimed. I would have chosen somewhere like the Plaza.

"I love coffee shops!" Mum replied. "Besides, we'll have lunch and dinner at smarter places.

30

Anyway, after breakfast we're going to go to the Metropolitan Museum of Art. Then we'll take a bus across Central Park and go to the Museum of Natural History. Then we'll make our way into town and go shopping. Everything will look so pretty for the holidays! Your dad and I will have to take you children there one December. Maybe next year. You'd love the decorations. A giant shimmery snowflake is suspended over Fifth Avenue. At Rockefeller Centre is the biggest Christmas tree you can imagine, and it's covered with tiny lights. And the windows of Saks—"

"Mum, Mum, I can't stand it," I interrupted. "Can't I go with you?"

"Sorry, darling," replied my mother. "Let's see. We're meeting the Sombergs for lunch and the four of us plan to try a new restaurant. In the afternoon, your dad and I will visit the Museum of Broadcasting and maybe walk around Lincoln Centre. Then we're going to meet the Wileys for dinner, and after *that* we're going to see *Phantom of the Opera*. Then we'll come home."

"Wow!" said Claire, who'd been listening. "Will you ever have time to go to the toilet?"

Leave it to Claire to make a connection between New York City and the toilet!

Mary Anne came over after dinner on Tuesday evening.

"Are you ready for two nights and a day at the Pike Zoo?" I asked her.

"No problem!" Mary Anne replied. "I'm a pro at this."

That was true. Mary Anne has come along as a mother's helper on a couple of Pike holidays. She can survive us for weeks at a time.

Mary Anne walked into our house and put her duffel bag on the floor. She called goodbye to her father, who had walked her over.

"Hello, Mary Anne-silly-billy-goo-goo!" cried Claire, running downstairs and wrapping her arms around Mary Anne's legs. "Silly-billy-goo-goo" is a term Claire attaches to the names of people she likes—when she's in her silly mood, which is fairly often.

Claire was followed by our brother Nicky, who's eight. "Crumble!" ordered Nicky, and Claire let go of Mary Anne and dropped to her hands and knees, tucking her head into her chest.

"What are they doing?" Mary Anne whispered to me.

"Nicky's told Claire he's got a special power over her," I whispered back. "Any time he tells her to crumble, she has to fall to the floor, no matter where she is or what she's doing. Nicky says he'll have this power forever, and that years from now, at Claire's wedding, he's going to wait till she's walking down the aisle and then he's going to whisper 'Crumble' to her."

Mary Anne smiled. But she didn't say anything about our family being a zoo till the triplets bounded down the stairs, pointing their fingers at Nicky and going, "Bzzzz!"

"Not the Bizzer Sign!" I muttered. I thought my brothers had forgotten about that. The Bizzer Sign is this annoying insult thing. They used to give each other the sign all the time. It never failed to annoy the younger children. Sure enough, Nicky turned to me with a pained expression and whined, "They're giving me the *Bizzer* Sign!"

"Good," said Claire. "My crumble's over then."

"It's not!" cried Nicky.

"It is too!"

"Children!" called Mum from the living room. "What's going on?"

"Nothing!" chorused Claire, Nicky, Byron, Adam, and Jordan. They turned and fled upstairs.

"Good move," I said to Mum. I led Mary Anne into the living room. "Here's Mary Anne," I added unnecessarily.

Mum and Dad were reading the newspaper. They smiled as we plopped onto the sofa.

It was time for . . . the Briefing. Mum and Dad were going to talk to us about our babysitting job. Dad had written out a sheet of instructions, reminders, notes, phone numbers, and addresses. He handed it to Mary Anne and me.

Even so, Mary Anne pulled a pen and a small notepad out of her bag and sat poised to take notes. (She's *such* a good secretary.)

"Let's see," Mum began. "First of all, Mary Anne, you'll be sharing Mal and Vanessa's room. We'll put a camp bed in there for you."

"We'd give you our room," added Dad, "but we'll be using it tonight, as well as after we come home tomorrow. You two haven't really got much of a night-time job. Mrs Pike and I will be away for less than twenty-four hours."

"Yes." All we have to do is look after seven children for the day," I said.

"They'll be at school for six hours," Mum pointed out.

"That's true."

"Anyway, Mallory," Mum continued, "Dad and I plan to get up at five tomorrow, drive to the station, and catch the six-thirty train. We're going to be hard to reach while we're away, but if there's a real emergency, you can call the Sombergs or the Wileys and they'll give us a message when they see us."

"Their phone numbers are on the sheet I gave you," said Dad.

"Besides," Mum went on, "several of the neighbours know we're going to be away tomorrow. So if you need help, you could call Mrs McGill or Mrs Barrett or the Braddocks—"

"Or my dad," added Mary Anne. "He'll be at home tomorrow night."

"Great," said Mum. "Now about meals—I desperately need to get some food in, but you've got enough for tomorrow. There's cereal and fruit for breakfast and enough things for scrambled eggs for dinner. I'll leave enough cash so that you can buy your lunches at school tomorrow and Thursday. There should also be enough food for Thursday morning's breakfast, and then I'll go to the shops as soon as I can that morning."

Mary Anne was taking down practically every word my parents said. She'd filled three pages on her little pad and had just started a fourth. (She's just a bit compulsive!)

"So," I said to Mum and Dad, "how much money are you going to leave us? Not that we'll need it for anything except school lunches, but you never know."

Mum handed over a bundle of notes. "I expect to get most of this back," she said.

I looked at the fortune in my hands. "Where am I going to keep this? We'd better have a good hiding place." I gave the money to Mary Anne. "Here, you hide it," I said. "I can't do it. I'm afraid I'll lose it."

Mary Anne took the money, Mum and Dad gave us a few more instructions, and then Mum said, "I think I'll go upstairs and have a talk with the triplets about the Bizzer Sign."

"I'll help you two put up the camp bed," said Dad to Mary Anne and me.

"Oh, we can do it!" I cried. "Come on, Mary Anne."

Mary Anne and I were busily wedging the camp bed between Vanessa's bed and mine, when Adam charged into the room.

"Don't bother knocking," said Vanessa, who was seated at her desk. She frowned, then added, "And please stop your mocking." (Vanessa wants to be a poet.)

"I haven't said anything!" exclaimed Adam. "Yet."

"What's the matter?" I asked. I thought maybe he was going to complain because Mum had talked to him and Byron and Jordan about the Bizzer Sign.

Adam grinned broadly. "Guess what I just heard on the news?" he said. Then he added meaningfully, "On WSTO."

I glanced at Mary Anne and shrugged.

Vanessa looked up long enough to say, "A war? A robbery? A traffic jam? A prisoner on the run?"

Adam made a face. "*No!* The weather man just said we're supposed to get a big snowstorm tomorrow."

What a tired old story. I put a striped pillow case on a pillow and arranged it on Mary Anne's bed.

"Hey, Vanessa," Adam went on, "you can put

away your homework. We won't be having any school tomorrow."

"Have you done yours yet?" Mary Anne asked Adam. "Because I wouldn't count on a snowy day."

"Most of it," Adam muttered. He left the room, looking gloomy.

But I felt great.

I caught Mary Anne's eye. Our adventure was about to begin!

5th CHAPTER

Stacey

Wednesday

Yea! No snow, no snow, no snow! I know most kids (probably most adults, too) start praying for snow the second a weather forecaster so much as says the word. But snow was the last thing I wanted on Wednesday, and since it had been predicted (again), I was pretty happy when, by the end of school that day, we were still snow-free. I could not wait to get home and bug Mum.

Mum had made a solemn promise. She had said I could get my hair permed for the Winter Wonderland Dance. It wouldn't be my first perm or anything, but I wanted a new one very badly. My old one looked a bit limp. It also *looked* like a perm. Do you want to know a beauty secret? Okay. The secret of good make-up and a good hairstyle is to look as if you haven't got any make-up on and you haven't had your hair styled. It may seem odd to spend money on make-up and hairdressers when your goal is to look as if you don't use them, but I suppose the idea is to seem natural. Anyway, I needed a perm so that I could look as if I didn't have one.

I was going to the dance with this boy called Austin Bentley. I've been out with him before and so has Claudia. We don't love him. He's just a nice boy. So I invited him to the dance. Even if he wasn't a *special* date, I wanted to look good on Friday. Getting my hair permed was important. So was going to Washington Shopping City.

Washington Shopping City is one of those huge shopping complexes that looks as if it's been dropped out of the sky and just happened to land in a carpark next to a motorway. It's enormous. In the arcade are shops, restaurants, even a cinema. Unfortunately, the arcade isn't in Stoneybrook. You have to drive for about half an hour to get there, if you take the motorway. If you take the back roads, the trip could be a lot longer.

Now, my mum's great, but one of her faults is that she's afraid to drive in snow. She had said we could go to the Shopping City for my perm *if* the roads were clear. The night before, when I'd heard the most recent WSTO weather forecast, I'd panicked. Snow for Wednesday! No way would Mum drive me to the arcade if a storm came. I'd have to settle on going to the local place on Thursday. And the local hairdresser's, Gloriana's House of Hair, isn't exactly wonderful. (You should have seen what Gloriana did to Kristy's stepsister once!)

Can you understand why I was jubilant when I left school on Wednesday and *no snow* was falling? The sky was overcast, almost leaden, and the temperature had dropped to 28 degrees, but—no snow! (The weather was stuck in a rut.)

"Mum, Mum!" I called as soon as I ran in the door after school.

"In the kitchen, dear," she replied.

I found my mother sitting at the kitchen table, paying bills. "It's not snowing," I announced.

Mum smiled. "You don't want to drive all the way out to the Shopping City, do you?"

"Yes!" I cried. "I do! You said we could if—" I realized Mum was teasing. "So we're still going?" I asked.

"Of course," replied my mother. She glanced outside. "I don't see why not."

"Oh, thank you, thank you! Can Claudia come with us?"

"Of course."

"Great!" I exclaimed. I grabbed the phone and dialled Claudia's personal number. (She's so lucky.) "Hi!" I said when Claudia answered. "It's me. We're still going to the mall. Want to come with us?"

"I do," replied Claudia, "but I'd better not. I don't think you'll be back in time. I'm sitting for the Perkinses tonight. And before that, I've got to take BSC phone calls, as we're not holding our meeting. Remember? I promised Kristy. She'd kill me if I skipped out to go to the arcade instead."

"Yes. Sorry. I forgot that you volunteered to take calls. Can I get you anything from the arcade?" (This was a dangerous question.)

"Just go and drool over the stuff in the jewellery shop, okay?"

I laughed. "Okay. Have fun at the Perkinses'. Call me when you get home."

"Okay," replied Claud. "See you."

I rang off and immediately Mum pounced on me. "Stacey? You'd better eat something before we leave." (As if you can't buy food in the arcade!) "And have you given yourself your insulin?"

For heaven's sake! I *am* thirteen. I've been coping with my diabetes for years now. (Well, for a couple of years.) But I understood Mum's concern. Some time ago, I *wasn't* careful about my diet—and I ended up in hospital.

"I won't need another injection for a couple of hours," I told Mum. "But I do need a snack. I'll eat in the car, though."

"Are you in a hurry?" teased Mum.

I laughed. "Come *on*. I want to get going."

I put an apple, some carrot sticks, and a handful of crackers in a bag. Then I hurried Mum out to the car.

As we sped along the motorway, I ate the apple and most of the crackers. I put the bag away and slid a cassette into the tape player.

The music came on.

I slid my eyes sideways, glancing at Mum. She was glancing at me.

"How come," I said, "this tape from a case labelled *Shout It*! by the Tin Can Voices is playing Vivaldi's *Four Seasons*?"

Mum raised her eyebrows. "Stacey, I'm impressed. You can recognize Vivaldi. I'll have to swap tapes more often."

"I suppose," I said, "that I'll find *Shout It*! in a Vivaldi case at home?"

"I wouldn't be surprised."

"Mum, this is cruelty to children," I protested. (We were laughing.)

I let Vivaldi play away. (Of course, Vivaldi him*self* wasn't playing. Vivaldi composed the music, but he's been dead for years.)

42

"Stacey, are you dressed warmly enough?" asked Mum out of the blue.

"You mean, considering the heater's blasting away and the windows are shut?" I replied. (The truth is, I *wasn't* dressed warmly enough for a 28-degree day. But I was overdressed for equatorial weather, which was how the inside of the car felt. Mum hasn't got a very good heater control.)

"Stacey," said my mother warningly.

I knew that if I uttered one more word, she would say something like, "How badly do you want to go to the arcade? Because we can always turn round and head for home."

"Sorry," I apologized. "Okay. I'm not dressed *quite* warmly enough, but I look good. Besides," I added quickly, seeing the expression on Mum's face, "we're hardly going to be outside at all. We just have to walk from the car into the arcade and back. I can manage that."

Mum sighed. I'm sure," she said, "that I never acted *any*thing like you when *I* was thirteen years old."

I leaned over and gave Mum a kiss on the cheek. "I love you," I said.

"I love you, too."

Washington Shopping City was, as Mum said, decorated to the hilt. For Christmas and Hanukkah, that is. She meant that it was over-

43

decorated, both inside and out. The first thing I noticed as we approached the Shopping City from the highway was this enormous neon Santa, a sleigh, eight reindeer, and Rudolph, perched on top of Sears department store. Not far away, running across the outside of another department store, was a menorah outlined in lightbulbs. And tinsel was everywhere. It looked as if an aluminium-foil factory had exploded.

We went inside. Not an inch of space was left undecorated. And in the centre of the arcade was a large gingerbread house, circled by a line of impatient children waiting to visit Santa Claus, who sat on a throne inside.

"Mummy, Mummy, can I go and see Santa?" I asked.

Mum smiled. "Maybe next year, dear," she replied. "Come along."

We reached the hairdresser's and luckily, Joyce, my favourite stylist, was free. Before long I was sitting in a chair, smelling like rotten eggs.

"Stace?" said Mum, who looked bored. "I'm going to pop in to Sears. Won't be long."

"Okay," I replied.

Joyce was hard at work. After a while, I was ready to "cook" under the hairdryer. Then Joyce unwound my rollers. Mum came back. She watched as Joyce combed my hair out.

"You look lovely, darling," said Mum.

44

"Thanks! And thank you for letting me have the perm. I really appreciate it. I hope you know that."

We were standing at the desk, and Mum was writing out a cheque, when another customer came into the salon. "Whew! It's really snowing!" she exclaimed.

I glanced at my mother. "Uh-oh!" I said.

6th CHAPTER

Kristy

Wednesday

I hardly ever see Bart during the week, just for fun. Sometimes I see him at softball practices or games, but that's about it. Films or anything spur-of-the-moment are reserved for weekends. But Wednesday was an exception, and I decided to make the most of it. Unfortunately, so did my little brothers and sisters.

It never occurred to me that a snowstorm would actually hit on Wednesday. If that had occurred to me, would I have invited Bart over? I have no idea.

Wednesday afternoon seemed strange. Well, it *was* a little strange. Unusual, anyway. Christmas was drawing near, so our house was decorated. Almost. Watson had strung lights on the fir tree in the front garden. Inside, evergreen branches were everywhere, along with our favourite old decorations. The only thing missing was the indoor tree. (We'd bought one; we just hadn't put it in the living room yet.) Also, as I mentioned before, Karen and Andrew were living with us for two weeks.

Most unusual, though, was . . . no BSC meeting. We've missed meetings here and there, but usually because my friends and I were away on holiday. Or because we were all busy with some school event or project. But that day was just a fairly ordinary Wednesday. I wondered what to do with myself. I had no sitting job and wasn't even needed to watch my younger brothers and sisters. So I got out my schoolbooks and did my homework. I finished early. Now what? An unexpected stretch of time lay before me.

The phone rang.

Bart! I thought, and dashed into the kitchen.

But the call was for Karen. Her friend Nancy wanted to know if Emily Junior had turned up. Very sadly, Karen admitted that she hadn't. When Karen got off the phone, I decided to ring Bart myself.

Wait! What was I going to say to him?

In an instant, one of my brilliant ideas slipped into my brain. If it was okay with Mum and Nannie and Watson, I would invite Bart over to watch a couple of videos, and then maybe he could stay for dinner.

I was in luck. I got permission, *and* Charlie volunteered to drive me to the video shop so that I could hire some tapes.

I rang Bart. "Want to come over?" I asked. "I thought we could watch some films. And Mum said you can stay for dinner."

"Today?" replied Bart.

"Yes."

"But it's Wednesday. It's a school day. And you've got a BSC meeting." Bart sounded horribly confused.

"There's no meeting," I told him. "It was cancelled. And you don't have to stay too late. Come on. It'll be fun. What sort of films do you like?"

"Oh, funny ones."

Of *course* Bart seemed confused. We'd been spending more time together recently, but mostly at weekends. I hardly ever rang him in an afternoon in the middle of the week. And I'd certainly never invited him to dinner. To be honest, I was slightly nervous about exposing him to my family, but I thought it might be time to do that. I mean, Bart's met everyone from Nannie to Emily Michelle; he's just never had a dose of the *entire* Brewer/Thomas household for any length of time.

I hoped he liked rats.

"Do you mind if Emily Junior's on the loose?" I asked.

Not surprisingly, Bart sounded taken aback. Still, he said, "Nope."

"Good. I'll ring you again when I get back from the video shop."

Ah. This seemed the perfect way to spend a cold, cloudy, almost-winter afternoon. Films, dinner, Bart.

Charlie drove me to the video shop, and after humming and hawing so long that my brother said, "Are you planning to hire something before Christmas?" I finally chose two films: *Uncle Buck* and *Back to the Future*.

I called Bart as soon as I was at home again.

"Come over," I said.

"Then I put the videos on top of the television in the study. It was at this point that I noticed something disturbing. Karen, Andrew, David Michael, and Emily Michelle weren't *doing* anything. They were hanging around the house, draping themselves over sofas and chairs, whining, complaining, and occasionally yelling at one another.

They were bored.

"Nannie," I said nervously, "the kids are bored."

Nannie sighed. "Well . . ." Her voice trailed off.

"Oh, please. I don't want them pestering us when—"

Ding-dong.

"—Bart's here," I finished.

And at that moment, eight little feet thundered towards the front door.

"I'll get it!" I screeched.

I ran for the door and edged the kids away.

"Who is it?" asked David Michael. "Is it your . . . boyfriend?"

My hand was on the door. I was all ready to open it for Bart, who was probably freezing. Instead, I turned around, put my other hand on my hip, and glared at the four kids. "Bart is *not* my boyfriend," I hissed.

"Should I tell him that?" asked David Michael.

"Don't you dare!"

Karen was peeping out of a window to make sure Bart was really the one who had rung the bell. (We are supposed to remember to do that so that we don't fling open the door and find a stranger on our doorstep.) "It *is* Bart . . . your boyfriend," she added devilishly.

"I know," I said.

"But you didn't check."

"But I was going to."

"Are you sure?"

"Nannie!" I yelled.

"What?" she replied.

"Your grandchildren are driving me mad!"

Nannie rescued me for the time being. She collected David Michael, Emily, Karen, and Andrew and took them upstairs to their playroom.

I was finally able to let poor Bart inside.

"Sorry about that," I told him. "Unfortunately, the kids are rather bored today."

"No problem," said Bart, who's pretty easygoing.

Bart and I settled into the study with a large bowl of popcorn. I slipped *Uncle Buck* into the VCR. I turned round. Bart was sitting more or less in the middle of the sofa, the popcorn next to him.

Well, now what? Where was I supposed to sit?

Was the popcorn an invitation to join Bart on the sofa? If I did that, I would have to sit *right next to him*. Would he think I was being too . . . forward? I could sit in the armchair, but then I wouldn't be near the popcorn. Bart would have to stretch halfway across the room to pass it to me.

I solved the problem by sitting on the floor near Bart's feet, as if that was where I always sat to watch films. Ten minutes later, Bart joined me on the floor. He sort of slid off the sofa—very casually—till he was sitting next to me. I reached back, found the popcorn bowl, and moved it to the floor, too. But I didn't reach for a handful till I saw Bart reach for one. Then I made sure our hands brushed against each other.

"Hee, hee, hee!"

I distinctly heard a giggle.

Sure enough, Andrew was peeping into the room. Then he ducked out. A moment later, Emily pranced in. Her nappy was unfastened on one side and trailing down her leg. She waved gaily at Bart and me, then plopped onto the floor, blocking our view of the set. Oh, perfect! I thought.

Of course, by then I'd snatched my hand out of the popcorn bowl. So had Bart. Andrew came back into the room, spotted the popcorn, and helped himself. He wriggled between Bart and me on the floor.

"What are you watching?" he asked. (He sprayed Bart's face with popcorn as he spoke.) "Can I watch, too?"

"You are," I muttered. Then I hoisted myself onto the sofa. Bart followed me, wiping bits of corn kernels off his cheek.

I sat stiffly during the rest of *Uncle Buck* and the first half of *Back to the Future*. Karen joined us in the study. Andrew left, then came back with about thirty-five Matchbox cars. Nannie found Emily and put a new nappy on her—right there on the floor, in front of Bart.

My brothers and sisters talked endlessly to

Bart, but I began to feel like the Tin Man in *The Wizard of Oz*—as if my jaw had rusted shut.

Back to the Future was nearly over when David Michael appeared in the doorway and announced, "Dinner's ready. Mum wants everyone to come to the table. That means you, Kristy. And your boyfriend."

I made a face at my brother.

Usually, my family eats meals at the big table in the kitchen. We had made an exception on Wednesday evening. In honour of Bart, Mum and Watson had set the table in the dining room. They had dimmed the lights and lit candles. I felt weirder than ever in that romantic setting with Bart on my left and Karen on my right, Watson jabbering about an antique sale he'd been to, Emily humming the theme from *Sesame Street*, and Karen checking under the table every five minutes for some sign of her missing rat.

Since I'm not noted for being quiet, Sam said, as Nannie and Charlie began to clear the table later, "What's the matter, Kristy? You aren't embarrassed, are you?"

And David Michael added, "Embarrassed about what? Her *boyfriend*?"

I glanced helplessly at my mother.

"David Michael," she said.

"Mum," he replied.

Emily knocked over her cup of milk.

I put my forehead in my hands.

And Karen jumped up, ran to a window, and exclaimed, "Hey, it's *really* snowing!"

7th CHAPTER

Jessi

Wednesday

I was prepared
for rehearsal. I had
been dancing my
legs off at home.
It wasn't that I
hadn't performed
in _The Nutcracker_
before. I had. But
I make a habit of
doing my absolute
best in any class,
rehearsal, or performance.
So on Wednesday,
I was thinking about
Clara and Fritz and
their godfather
Drosselmeier, not

snow or icy roads or Quint. (Well, I was thinking about Quint a little bit.)

I was one of the BSC members who would have had to miss the Wednesday meeting if Kristy had decided to hold it. My ballet lessons are very important to me. And so are the productions I dance in. I've performed parts in *The Nutcracker* many times, but this was the first year I was cast as the King of the Mice. Usually, a boy plays that part, but I didn't mind doing it—once.

The Wednesday rehearsal was very important. Opening night was less than a week away, and every year *The Nutcracker* is the most attended ballet put on by my school. By my ballet school, that is. The special dance school I go to in Stamford. My teacher is Mme Noelle, and she works her pupils *hard*. There's no messing around in Madame's classes.

That was how I managed to concentrate so well on Wednesday. I *wanted* to think about Quint. And under any other circumstances, I would have done so, nonstop. I couldn't believe that in a few short hours I would be seeing him again. And the visit would be a long one.

I suppose I should explain a little. (I'm even confusing myself!) Quint and I met in New York when the members of the BSC were there for two wonderful weeks of summer holiday. Quint's a ballet dancer too, and we met at the ballet. We had each gone to a special matinée performance of *Swan Lake* at Lincoln Centre. We had gone alone—and we ended up sitting next to each other. Then we started talking. And finally we spent some time together. I met Quint's family, and I learned about Quint's dilemma. This was the thing. Quint is *such* a good dancer that his teacher thought he could be accepted at Julliard, which is the performing arts school in New York City. Not just anyone can get into it. You have to audition and you have to be *good*. Quint didn't want to audition; not because he thought he wouldn't get in, but because he was afraid he *would* get in! You see, the guys in Quint's neighbourhood had been giving him a hard time about taking ballet lessons. (Quint used to sneak off to lessons with his shoes and things stuffed into a bowling ball bag.) Anyway, Quint and I talked a lot while I was in New York, and finally he decided just to *see* if he could get into Julliard. So he auditioned, he got in (naturally), and he decided to go. The boys still give him a hard time, but he just puts up with that. He doesn't even bother to use the bowling bag any more.

I'm extremely proud of Quint. And I miss him. I haven't seen him since we said goodbye in NYC. (Oh, by the way, Quint kissed me then. My first kiss. My first meaningful kiss, that is.) We've

57

kept in touch, though, mostly by post. We write to each other almost every day. Not necessarily a long letter, but a note or a postcard. Or sometimes I'll find a cartoon or an ad or anything funny, and I'll just drop it in an envelope and address it to Quint. We've spoken on the phone, too. That was how we'd made the arrangements for Quint to come to Stoneybrook for the first time.

And to be my partner on the night of the Winter Wonderland Dance.

While I was at the Wednesday rehearsal for *The Nutcracker*, Quint was on a train roaring towards Stamford. The train was supposed to get in just a few minutes before the end of my rehearsal. My dad was going to pick up first Quint and then me. After that, Quint was going to come back to Stoneybrook with us and stay until Saturday. We would go to the dance and still have time for a good long visit, and for Quint to get to know Mama and Daddy; my little sister, Becca; my baby brother, Squirt; and my Aunt Ceceila (Daddy's sister, who lives with us).

With the prospect of seeing Quint at the end of rehearsal, are you surprised I was able to concentrate at *all*? I was surprised. But Mme Noelle is very compelling. She really captures your attention. Even so, my mind wandered a few times, and I found myself hoping that my carefully laid plans would be carried out without any trouble. I hoped Quint's train would be on time. I

58

hoped my rehearsal would end on time. I hoped
Daddy wouldn't get delayed on his way into the
city. Daddy usually works in Stamford. (That was
why we moved to Connecticut in the first place.
The company Daddy works for transferred his
job from New Jersey to Connecticut. Soon after
we moved, I met my friends in the Babysitters
Club.) On that Wednesday, however, Daddy had
to go to a meeting in Stoneybrook! He planned to
return to Stamford, though, after the meeting and
pick up Quint and me.

"Doncers! Eyes to ze front!" demanded Mme
Noelle. She stood before us in the big rehearsal
room at our school. Several assistant teachers
were spread among the doncers. (In case you
couldn't tell, Mme Noelle is French, and she
speaks with an accent.)

The doncers straightened up. But a couple of
the younger children were having some trouble
concentrating for so long.

I nudged one of them, an eight-year-old girl
called Sadie something. (I don't know the
younger dancers all that well. They're not in my
class, so I only see them at rehearsals or
performances.) "Pay attention," I whispered to
Sadie.

"But it's supposed to snow," she replied.

"Not a chance," I told her.

"The weatherman *said*."

Someone nudged me. "Jessi! Mme Noelle's

59

staring at you." It was Katie Beth, a friend from my ballet class.

I braced myself for the sound of "Mademoiselle Ramsey!" But it didn't come. The school secretary had tiptoed into the room and was whispering to one of the assistants, Mme Duprès. Mme Duprès frowned, nodded, signalled for Mme Noelle's attention, then whispered something to *her*.

Around me, Sadie and three other eight-year-olds (playing mice who fight alongside me, the Mouse King) sat on the floor, giggling.

"Come on, you lot. Stand up," I said. "The rehearsal isn't over."

"But my feet hurt," said Sadie.

"Mine, too," complained Danny.

"Mine, three," added Marcus and Wendy at the same time.

I couldn't blame them. The rehearsals had been growing longer and longer. The Wednesday rehearsal wasn't going to end until early evening. (So that no one would faint from starvation, the school kitchen had been stocked with crackers, packets of instant soup, and bags of dried fruit.)

Mme Noelle and Mme Duprès finished their conversation. Mme Duprès stepped back. I noticed that the secretary was still hovering in the doorway.

"*Mesdemoiselles et monsieurs*," said Mme Noelle, clapping her hands for attention. (I decided she'd forgotten I'd been talking to Sadie during class.)

60

"I have just been eenformed zat eet eez snowing—"

"Yea!" shouted Sadie. She struck at the air with her fist and added, "Yes!" Then she realized that the rest of the class was silent—and staring at her. "Sorry," she said, glancing helplessly at me.

"Apparently," Madame continued, "zee snow eez falling hard. Several of your parents have phoned to say zat zey are on zee way, or zat zey are *try*ing to be on zee way, but zat zey have been delayed."

"Huh?" said Danny.

"Who's delayed?" asked Wendy.

"Can I see the snow?" cried a six-year-old. Without waiting for an answer, she streaked out of the room and across the hallway to a window, stood on her tiptoes, and peered out. "Ooh, it *is* snowing!" she exclaimed. "I can't even see the street."

I glanced at the clock in the back of the room. We were supposed to rehearse for almost another hour. Even so, parents of some of the younger dancers would have arrived by this time, planning to watch the end of rehearsal.

But no parents were here yet.

Forty-five minutes later, still no parents had arrived, although several more had phoned, saying that they were stuck somewhere, were held up, etc. One of the parents who had phoned was Daddy. His meeting was over, he said, but he was

61

having trouble getting out of the car park. (Something to do with a stalled car.) He would be here as soon as he could.

At this point, Mme Noelle must have sensed that she was losing our attention, especially the attention of the younger kids. "All right. Rehearsal eez over," she announced. "You may change your clothes."

We scrambled for the changing rooms. (No parents turned up.) We changed our clothes. (No parents.) We stared outside at the whirling snow. (No parents.) Quint's train must have reached Stamford by now, I thought. And Daddy probably wasn't there to meet it. What was Quint doing?

I shivered. Suddenly I had a very bad feeling about the snow.

8th CHAPTER

Mary Anne

Wednesday

It finally snowed. No one could believe it. Even the weather forecasters seemed surprised. (Well, they'd been wrong for weeks. Predicting something that actually happened must have come as a shock to them.)

The snow didn't start until dinnertime, though, so it was a good thing the Pike kids had done their homework the night before. That morning, it was off to school as usual, for everyone except me.

What I mean is, it was off to school for me, too; it's just that it wasn't off as usual. "Off as usual" would have meant waking up in my own room and leaving from my own house. But on Wednesday, I left from the Pikes', having woken up jammed into the bedroom that Mallory and Vanessa share.

It was very early. I woke to the sounds of people trying to be quiet. There's nothing quite as disturbing as people who are *trying* to be quiet so they won't wake up other people, the ones who are sleeping. Mr and Mrs Pike were up long before the rest of us. They got up even before their alarm went off. Since Mal and her brothers and sisters and I didn't have to get up till after the Pikes had left, Mr and Mrs Pike were trying valiantly to let us sleep. Consequently, I could hear lots of whispers. Things like, "Shhh! Don't disturb the kids!" and, "Turn down the radio! You're going to wake the whole neighbourhood." Then I heard somebody tiptoe, tiptoe, and *crash*! into something he couldn't see because he hadn't turned on a light.

I never did go back to sleep. I lay on the camp bed and listened to the sounds of Mr and Mrs Pike making coffee, then warming up the car in the chilly garage, and finally leaving for the railway station. I listened to Vanessa snoring lightly. I listened to Mal, who kept turning over and over in her bed. (She sleeps like an eggbeater.)

Finally I heard the clock radio go off somewhere in the house. Then another one. Seconds later, a third went off practically in my ear.

"*There she was just a walkin' down the street, singin' do-wah-ditty-ditty-dum-ditty-do,*" blasted the radio.

"Oh!" groaned Mal.

Vanessa woke up smiling. "*She looks good,*" she chimed in with the song. "*She looks fine. And I'm happy that she's mine.*"

"'Morning, Vanessa!" I said. "Hey, Mal! Come on. Let's get going."

"Do-wah," said Mal.

Apparently, the Pikes had tuned all the radios in the house to the same oldies station. By the time I knocked on the door to the boys' room, a new song had come on. Nicky swung open the door and burst into the hallway, holding a hairbrush to his mouth, singing, "*Who put the bop in the bop-shoo-bop-shoo-bop?*" Seconds later, from the third bedroom, came the sound of Margo and Claire belting out, "*Who put the ram in the rama-lama-ding-dong?*"

By breakfast time, the eight kids and I were singing, "*Lollipop, lollipop, ooh-la-la-lolli-lollilol-lipop, lollipop, ooh-la-la . . .*"

"That's what I'd like for breakfast," said Margo, sliding into her place at the kitchen table. "A big orange lollipop. No, a purple one."

"Well, today's breakfast is toast and cereal and

65

bananas. We haven't got any lollipops. Sorry," I said.

"Bother!" replied Margo.

"Can I have a Popsicle?" asked Byron.

"A Popsicle?" I repeated. The Pike kids *are* allowed to eat pretty much whatever they want, but chocolate ice cream for breakfast? "I suppose so," I said anyway. I looked at Mal, who shrugged.

"That's okay," said Byron. "I don't really want one. I just wanted to know if I could have one." He glanced out of the window. "So much for the snow," he added.

"We're *never* going to get any snow," whined Vanessa.

"You say that every year," said Adam.

"Let's listen to a weather report," suggested Jordan.

When one came on a few minutes later, Mallory snorted. "*Heavy* snow?" she repeated. "Now they're saying *heavy* snow?"

"Maybe it'll start this morning," said Nicky hopefully, "and school will close early and we'll leave before they give out any work."

"Maybe," I said, but when Mal and I left Claire, Margo, Nicky, Vanessa, and the triplets at Stoneybrook Elementary School, the sky was as relentlessly snow-free as ever, although the air *was* colder and damper than usual.

We said goodbye to the kids and Mal called, "Remember, Claire. Two sessions of kindergarten today. Stay with your teacher until we come for you in the afternoon." (Claire usually goes to morning kindergarten, but that day she would stay for the second session as well, and then Mal and I would pick her up at the same time as we picked up the other Pike children.)

Nicky didn't get his wish for an early closing of school. By the time the Pikes and I reached their house that afternoon, Mallory was actually laughing at the weather forecasters. "They said heavy snow developing quickly and starting before noon," she said, giggling. "Well, it's gone three now."

"Perhaps the forecast's a few hours out," said Jordan. "It could still snow."

"Yes," agreed Byron, "especially if we do a snow dance."

"A what?" I asked.

"A snow dance. You know, like a rain dance. Only to make snow come."

"Let's do one now!" cried Vanessa.

"But you've just taken off your coats," said Mal.

"We'll put them back on," replied Adam.

A few minutes later, Mallory and I were standing in the back garden watching her sisters and brothers stamp around, chanting, "Hey, come on, make it snow! Make it snow! Do-wah-ditty-ditty-dum-ditty-doe!"

At four o'clock, we called them inside. "Time to begin your homework," I said.

The triplets made faces. "I *know* we're not going to have school tomorrow," said Byron, but he didn't look as certain as he sounded.

Nevertheless, the boys began their homework, the radio playing in the background.

"Couldn't you think better with that off?" Mal asked them.

"We're listening for school closings," Jordan told her.

"But it *isn't snowing*," said Mal.

"*But it will be*," Nicky replied through clenched teeth.

Mallory sighed.

By six o'clock, we had finished our homework.

"Dinner!" Mal announced.

"What are you making?" asked Margo.

"Scrambled eggs. You lot lay the table while Mary Anne and I cook, okay?"

By the time we sat down to eat, the children had finally given up on the snow. They sat glumly around the table, pushing their food around their plates.

Claire got up to pour herself another glass of milk. As she passed the window, she let out a yelp. "It's snowing!" she exclaimed.

"Very funny," mumbled Adam.

"No, really! It *is* snowing. Honest."

Every single person in the kitchen jumped up

68

and joined Claire at the window. Sure enough, tiny flakes were falling. They were quite hard to see, though.

"We'll probably get a few centimetres," I said.

"Do they close school for a few centimetres?" asked Nicky.

"No, twit," Jordan said witheringly to his brother. "Anyway, I bet it's just a flurry."

The snow was still falling when we began to clear the table.

"You know, it's starting to fall harder," I said to Mal.

"It's sticking," she added.

"Can we play in it?" asked Nicky. "Before it melts?"

"Why not?" replied Mal. "You've done your homework."

Once again, the kids dressed to go outdoors. Only now they added boots and waterproof trousers to their outfits. I turned on the light in the back garden. "Stay away from the road!" I called as the Pikes hurtled outside.

The snow was not only sticking, it was beginning to pile up. And it was falling thickly. I couldn't see very far in front of me. "Do you suppose the weatherman was finally right?" I asked Mal.

"I suppose he had to be some time," she replied.

"Yum, tasty snow!" exclaimed Claire. She was

walking around with her tongue sticking out, catching flakes on it. "Mmm. Mint-flavoured."

Vanessa stuck out her tongue, too. "Mine's cherry. Very cherry."

"You girls are crazy," pronounced Nicky. Then he shouted. "Crumble!" to Claire, who obeyed.

Pow! A snowball exploded against Nicky's back.

"No snowball fights!" yelled Mallory.

"Drat!" replied Adam. Then he turned to his little sister. "Hey, Claire, did you know that if we get enough snow, the Abominable Snowman appears?"

"Does he?" answered Claire.

"Yup. He rises out of the snow in the garden. Then he comes into the house and turns children under six into Popsicles."

"Oh, yeah?" replied Claire. "How can he come inside? He'd melt."

"Not the *Abominable* Snowman. He's magic," Adam told her.

"You mean like Frosty?"

"Yes. Only Frosty's nice and the Abominable Snowman's . . . a monster."

"Yikes!" shrieked Claire.

"Okay, okay. I think it's time to go in," I said. The snow wasn't showing any signs of stopping; besides, I didn't want the Abominable Snowman story to get out of hand. "Come on, everybody."

70

Inside, Mal and I helped the younger children take off their wet clothes. We draped damp mittens and hats around the laundry room. Then we threw wet socks into the tumble dryer. After that, Mal made hot chocolate and we sat round the kitchen table with steaming mugs in front of us.

"You know, school might be closed tomorrow, after all," I said.

"We did our homework for nothing then," said Nicky, pouting.

"For nothing?! Hey, you'll have a free day tomorrow," Mal told her brother.

"Well, *I* didn't have any homework anyway," said Claire smugly.

"That's good," replied Adam, "because the Abominable Snowman also steals homework."

9th CHAPTER

Dawn

Wednesday Evening

The drive to the airport was totally scary. Even though I can't drive, and even though I was sitting in the front seat, I turned into an awful backseat driver. I thought Mum was going to throw me out of the car. "Dawn!" she kept saying. "Relax!" Which isn't very relaxing when someone is screeching the words in your ear, and at the same time gripping the steering wheel so tightly her knuckles had probably turned white (she was wearing gloves, so I couldn't tell for sure), and then leaning forward so her nose was an eighth of an inch from the windshield...

When I got home from school on Wednesday, I found my mum in a nervous state, which isn't very comforting to a thirteen-year-old. I knew something was wrong when I walked in the door and found Mum dusting the living room. The fact that she was at home during the day wasn't so odd. Mum works, but she'd told me earlier that she'd arranged to take this day off. The odd thing was that she was dusting. My mum is *not* a cleaner. Or a washer or a cooker or a sewer (as in "person who sews", not as in "smelly underground tunnel"). She can *do* those things all right, but she would prefer not to. Mary Anne's dad is the organized, domestic adult in the family. Mum's a scatterbrain who would do just about anything rather than pick up a duster.

"What's wrong?" I asked Mum, closing the front door behind me.

Mum looked up. I don't think she'd heard the door open.

"Hi, darling," she said. "I don't know. I don't like the sound of the weather report."

"What's the report?"

"For heavy snow."

"Oh, Mum. They've been saying that for days now. Have you seen a single flake of snow? Have you even seen a drop of *rain*?"

"No," she admitted.

"Besides, what's so bad about snow?" I meant, what's so bad about it apart from the fact that it's

73

freezing cold and wet? As a California girl, I'm hardly ever warm enough in Connecticut. California may not be the tropics. It has its share of cold, damp weather, but nothing like Connecticut's freezing winters. And I'd certainly never seen snow where I lived in California. Winter in the East had been quite a shock.

However, my mother had grown up in Stoneybrook. "You used to drive in snow all the time, Mum," I pointed out.

"Yes, but I didn't like it. California was a huge relief."

"Well, think about Jeff instead."

"I have been. This isn't good flying weather."

"He doesn't get airsick."

"He gets scared, though."

I sighed. Every now and then I feel as if I'm my mother's mother. "In a few hours he'll be here, your worrying will be over, and we'll start a wonderful winter holiday," I said. "I'm really excited."

Finally Mum smiled. "I am, too. And bored. I've finished dusting." (She'd dusted one end table and a couple of chair legs.)

Guess what? By the time we left for the airport, it was *snowing*. I couldn't believe it. The weather forecast had actually been right. (Well, I suppose in Connecticut, if you keep predicting snow, you're bound to be right occasionally.)

74

Mum was a nervous wreck.

"Why don't I go to the airport with you?" Richard asked Mum. (Richard is Mary Anne's father.)

"Oh, darling, that's okay," said Mum. (If Mary Anne had been at home, she and I would have exchanged a smile. We always do when we hear our parents call each other "dear" or "darling" or something. Jeff just says, "Gross!") "I'm sure we'll be fine. I should get used to snow again. Besides, you promised Mary Anne you'd be at home in case she or Mallory needs you."

"Are you sure?" asked Richard.

"Positive." Mum smiled. (Sort of.)

So we set off. Mum had insisted on leaving ages before Jeff's plane was due in. As it turned out, that was a good move. Mum backed down the drive at a crawl, then edged onto the road. Okay, so it was snowing a little. A couple of centimetres had settled on the ground. But I couldn't see what the big deal was. Surely she could speed up to, oh, ten miles an hour.

No way. It turned out Mum knew what she was doing. As she crept towards the stop sign at the end of our street (which took about twenty minutes) I felt her put on the brakes—very gently. And the next thing I knew, our car was slipping eerily to the right, to the left, and to the right again. I looked around frantically, trying to see what we might crash into—the stop sign, a

Dawn

postbox, a telegraph pole. Is this it? I wondered. Is this how I'm going to die? By sliding, on a couple of centimetres of snow at five miles an hour, into the Bahadurians' postbox? (Which, by the way is shaped like a cow.)

Well, we did run into the cow postbox, but as we were moving so slowly, we barely scraped it. In fact, we touched it just hard enough so that some of the snow that had landed on the cow's head showered to the ground.

Nevertheless, I heard Mum say a word I've never heard her use before. In fact, I've only heard it in films that Mum doesn't know I've seen.

"Mum!" I gasped. I was more stunned by what she'd said than by the fact that we'd had an accident while our house was still in view.

"Sorry, darling," she murmured. She straightened up the car, and soon we were on our way again, Mum all tight-lipped and gripping the steering wheel. Once we reached a main road, the driving wasn't quite so horrible. As the snow fell, it was turned to slush by the wheels of the cars that ground over it. The slush wasn't as slippery as the unploughed snow. The road wasn't as dark either. It was lit by street lamps.

"The motorway will be a piece of cake," I said to Mum.

Wrong. The snow was falling more thickly by the time Mum inched onto the motorway. And

76

there weren't as many cars on the motorway as there had been in Stoneybrook itself. The few cars that did come by were creeping along like Mum. This was when I turned into a backseat driver.

"It's getting windy," I murmured, as flakes swirled across our headlights. "Go slowly, Mum."

"Right."

"And the snow's sticking. No slush."

Grimly, Mum drove on.

"We could turn round," I said in a small voice.

"Go back?" replied Mum. She shook her head. "Jeff would be stranded at the airport. Then he'd *really* feel abandoned."

"Oh, yes."

We continued in silence. Finally, I glanced at my watch. "Hey, we're late!" I exclaimed. "At least, we're going to be late."

Mum shook her head. "All we can do is keep moving. Jeff will wait for us. He'll probably ring Richard."

"And Richard will tell him how long ago we left the house and then Jeff will think we've been in an accident."

"Dawn, I—"

"Mum, look out!" I screamed.

On the other side of the motorway, the headlights of a huge lorry wavered as its wheels skidded. Then the lorry bumped off the motorway, heading for the snow-covered central reservation —and for our car.

I covered my eyes with my hands and prayed that my seat belt would do whatever it was supposed to do. A second later I felt our car swerve.

Then Mum said that word again.

I dared to open my eyes.

Somehow, the lorry was back where it belonged. It was still slewed across the central reservation. It had run into the car in front of it (and we had nearly run into a van in the right lane), but I didn't think anyone was hurt. I could see the drivers of the lorry and the car opening their doors and climbing out to examine the damage.

"A fender bender," said Mum through clench-ed teeth.

"Oh, my lord!" I muttered. "I thought we were dead." I started to shake and couldn't stop, even though Mum turned up the heat.

During the rest of the torturous drive I could do nothing but look at the cars around us and yelp for Mum to be careful. Also, I kept announcing how late we were. "Jeff's plane landed ten minutes ago." . . . "Jeff's plane landed fifteen minutes ago."

"Dawn, I'm doing my best," said Mum. "Just relax."

"Jeff's going to be panicking!" I cried.

No answer.

Somehow, we reached the airport. Mum found a parking spot near the entrance. (The carpark was practically empty.) Then we hurried inside. Mum had phoned the airport before we left, so she knew the gate where Jeff's plane had landed.

I grabbed her hand. "Come on!" I said, and we raced through the airport.

10th CHAPTER

Stacey

Wednesday Evening

My hair looked great. It really did. Joyce had performed a miracle. (Mum gave her a big tip.) I was so enthralled with it that I looked at myself in every mirror between the salon and the exit to the parking lot. I barely even thought about the snow. A few minutes later, everything had changed around. My hair was forgotten and I could think of nothing but the snow. And my mum. It is not fun to be a kid watching your mother become frightened.

To be honest, I'm not sure whether Mum tipped Joyce so well because of the good work she'd done or because Mum was distracted by the woman who'd come into the salon and announced that it was snowing. It could have been the snow since, as I mentioned, my mother isn't very experienced at driving in it. At any rate, Joyce looked very pleased with her tip.

Mum rushed me out of the salon before I'd even put on my coat.

"Hurry up, darling," she said.

"Let me get my coat on."

"You can do that while we're walking."

Walking? Huh! Mum dragged me through the arcade at sixty miles an hour. We were moving so fast that I hadn't even managed to shrug into my jacket by the time we reached the exit.

Mum frowned as she waited for me to do my zip up.

"What?" I exclaimed, exasperated. "You want me to go out in that with no jacket?" Then I just *had* to cover my head so my wonderful new perm wouldn't get wet.

I thought Mum would have a fit.

But I forgot about my hair, my jacket, everything, the second Mum opened the door. When she did so, a gust of snow blasted us. That's how fast the snow was moving: it actually hurt our faces.

I thought Mum would close the door and come

straight back inside. But no, she set her jaw and continued towards the car. I hustled behind her, shielding my eyes from the stinging snowflakes.

We found the car, which was a wonder. The car park was full of snow-covered lumps. How Mum could tell our snow-covered lump from all the others is beyond me, but she could. She aimed right for it. She must be equipped with special Mother Radar.

In a flash she had unlocked the doors, and we were sitting in the car with the defroster and the windshield wipers going. The wipers weren't strong enough to clear the windows, though. Mum had to get out and work on them from the outside with an ice scraper. Then she slid into the driver's seat again.

She turned to look at me. "Ready?" she asked.

"I suppose so." I removed the scarf from my head and shook out my hair.

"Phew!" exclaimed Mum as she turned the key in the ignition. "Your hair—"

"I know. My hair smells like rotten eggs."

"Well . . . yes."

I giggled. "I thought mums were supposed to be supportive."

"Oh, we are, we are." My mother started the car, and we pulled out of our parking place and inched through the car park to the exit.

"Are you okay?" I asked Mum. She was

hunched over the steering wheel, leaning forward to peer through the windscreen.

Mum nodded. "It's hard to see, that's all."

We reached the end of the ramp leading to the motorway, and Mum looked over her shoulder. She looked for so long that I finally said, "Ahem!"

"I still can't see very well, Stace. The snow's awfully thick."

"Oh. I don't mind if we go slowly."

Mum eased onto the motorway. "Not bad!" she exclaimed a few moments later. "The motorway's clearer than the other roads were. I think we'll make it."

"Yes. We're survivors," I said seriously. "Intrepid snow explorers. We should be written up for 'Drama in Real Life', and our story should appear in *Reader's Digest*. Don't you think?"

Mum smiled. "Let's see. The title would read, um . . . 'BLIZZARD!'"

"Yes," I agreed. "'BLIZZARD!' And the story would tell how these two gorgeous young women—"

"Thank you, thank you," interrupted Mum.

"—who have just spent a gruelling afternoon shopping and getting their hair permed, climb into the family car—"

I stopped short.

Which is exactly what the car in front of us had done. With no warning, it just stopped. I mean,

83

its brake lights flashed on, but only a split second before the car stopped moving. Instinctively, Mum slammed on her brakes.

We skidded across the road.

I screamed. (I couldn't help it.)

"Stacey, be *quiet*!" said Mum, but I don't think she was aware that she'd spoken.

I was sure we were going to slide right into another car, or that another car was going to slide into us.

But that didn't happen. We came to a stop in the left-hand lane. I rubbed away the frost on my window and tried to see why the driver of the other car had slammed on his brakes. But I couldn't make out anything through the snow.

"That does it!" said my mother.

"What do you mean?"

"We're getting off the motorway. We'll take the back roads home."

"Why?"

"Because there are too many cars on the motorway. Too many mad drivers. There are probably accidents everywhere. I don't want us to find ourselves in the middle of a pile-up." Mum began to guide the car across the motorway, back to the right-hand lane. "We'll get off at the next exit," she said.

"Are you sure you know the way from here?" I asked.

"Yup," replied Mum. "Stop worrying, darling. I'll get us home safely."

We passed two fender benders before we reached the exit. "Look," Mum said. "We don't want to end up in one of those situations."

"Boy, I'm glad Claudia didn't come with us. We'd never have been back in time for her to sit at the Perkinses' house tonight."

My mum almost drove past the next exit ramp. Not that it would have made much difference, since she was going so slowly. At any rate, she did turn onto it and soon we were travelling through the countryside. (At least, I think that's what we were travelling through. I couldn't see anything except snow.)

"I suppose the weatherman was right after all," Mum commented.

"What? Oh, yes. I suppose he was . . . Mum, are you *positive* you know how to get home from here? I mean, are you absolutely positive?"

Mum gave me a Look. "Stacey, we're not lost," she said.

"Well, do you know where we are?"

"Darling, if I didn't know where we *were* then I wouldn't know where to *go*. Relax, okay? Haven't you got something to do?"

"You mean, did I remember to bring along a colouring book and crayons?"

Mum laughed. "Sorry. I'm feeling nervous. Put on a tape or turn on the radio, okay?"

"No problem." I turned on the radio, and tuned it to a rock station I love. Two songs belted out before I said, "Don't you want the classical station, Mum?" She was concentrating so hard on driving that she didn't hear me.

After several more minutes passed she said, "This snow's really *thick*. It's sticking, too. There are already several centimetres on the road."

I didn't know whether to feel glad because undoubtedly this meant . . . NO SCHOOL the next day! Or to feel worried because there we were, on some dark back road in the middle of nowhere, being practically buried by snow.

"Do you think this is a blizzard?" I asked.

Mum shook her head. (I think she meant to say, "I don't know.")

I stared outside, gazing at the storm. I remembered snowstorms in New York. I remembered watching the flakes whirl past my bedroom window. Sometimes the wind swept them *up* in a funnel.

"It's really coming down," my mother would say then.

"It's really going up," my father would say.

I was thinking about city blizzards when I realized that Mum had stopped the car.

"What's wrong? What are you doing?" I asked. (For some reason, I felt panicky immediately. *My* radar was picking up signals. My Kid Radar.)

"I think I'd better wait till the snow lets up a bit," Mum replied. "It's just too thick at the moment. I can't see more than a metre or so in front of me." She had stopped by the side of the road.

One thing I didn't worry about was being hit by some unsuspecting car from behind. This was because, for one thing, we hadn't seen a single car or van or even a pedestrian since we'd left the motorway. For another thing, Mum left our headlights on so that we *could* be seen. She also left on the heater. We would have turned to icicles without it.

Mum and I chatted and pretended we weren't the least bit nervous about what was happening. I kept looking at my watch and saying things like, "In ten minutes we should be on our way again."

When half an hour had passed, Mum resolutely turned on the ignition again. "The snow isn't any lighter," she said. "Well, all right. I'll just drive again. We'll reconcile ourselves to a long trip home, that's all."

Mum put her foot on the accelerator. She pressed down. She pressed harder.

I could feel our back wheels spinning.

Mum groaned. Then, as if she were moving in slow motion, she leaned forward until her head was resting on the steering wheel. "This isn't happening," she muttered.

My stomach turned to a block of ice. "Now what?" I asked.

Mum gathered herself together. "I'll try to move the car," she replied. Which was quite ridiculous because she wouldn't let me work the accelerator while she pushed the car, and she also wouldn't let me get out and push.

"I don't want you to get hurt," she said.

Mum rocked the car a few times, then rushed around and tried to drive us out of the snowy rut our wheels had created. It was no use.

We were stuck.

We were stranded!

11th CHAPTER

Kristy

Wednesday Evening

I thought the afternoon with Bart and my family had been excruciating. That was just because the evening hadn't happened yet. Oh, I know my disastrous adventure was nothing compared to, say, Stacey's, but it was a disaster on a different level.... Well, it was.

Okay, it sort of was.

"Liar!" cried David Michael.

Karen was still standing at the window. "I am *not* a liar!" she said indignantly. "It really is snowing. Come and look."

"Huh! I'm not falling for that," said my brother. "That's like telling someone his shoe's untied when he's wearing loafers."

Karen paused. Then she hissed, "David Michael, XYZ. Your fly's open!"

David Michael went red as a beetroot. He looked down, then up. "No, it isn't!" he exclaimed.

"Gotcha!" cried Karen. "Now come and look at the snow. I'm not kidding. I bet school will be closed tomorrow."

I put my head in my hands. Why did Karen have to go and mention *flies* in front of Bart? To make things worse, Bart leaned over to me and whispered, "What does XYZ mean?"

Karen heard him.

"It means 'examine your zip'!" she called from across the room. "Get it? X-amine Your Zip? XYZ?"

Oh, please. Somebody put me out of my misery.

David Michael did, although he wasn't aware of it. He shouted, "Hey, Karen's telling the truth! It *is* snowing!"

This started a stampede to the dining room windows. Even I looked.

"A real storm," said Charlie admiringly.

"I'm going to turn on the radio," announced Sam. And he did. He tuned the little kitchen radio to WSTO while we cleared the dining room table. As we carried plates and dishes to and fro, we heard one of the weather forecasters say, "Well, the storm *has* hit us. Better late than never! You can expect half a metre or more of snow before this blows over!" He sounded jubilant. I think he was pleased with his prediction.

"Half a metre!" repeated David Michael, awestruck.

"I wouldn't count on it," said Watson. He flicked off the radio. "We rarely get snow like that. We're too close to the sea."

"Oh, bullfrogs," said Karen.

"Maybe I should go home now," Bart spoke up.

"Why don't you wait a bit?" Watson replied. "Until it lets up a little. I don't really want to drive in that."

"Oh, I can walk," Bart assured him. (The Taylors live close by.)

"Oh, no," said Mum. "In the dark? In the wind?" (You'd think we lived in Alaska or somewhere.)

"I'm tough!" Bart joked.

"Seriously, just wait half an hour or so," said Watson. "Then I'll drive you."

"Is that all right with your parents?" asked Mum. "Can you stay a little longer? When are they expecting you home?"

"Not for a while," said Bart cheerfully.

"Great. Let's have dessert, then." Sam had opened the fridge door. He more or less lives in the fridge. He knows its contents by heart. "I hope that pie's still in the freezer," he said, and opened the freezer compartment to check. Sure enough, there was the pie. Shop bought, frozen, blueberry. "Won't this be excellent with vanilla ice cream?" Sam went on. (Of course, there was ice cream, too. It was behind the pie, where no one could see it, but Sam sensed its presence.)

Nannie put the pie in the microwave while Charlie and I set out plates, spoons, forks, and recycled paper napkins. Bart and my family and I ate warm blueberry pie and ice cream in the kitchen. It was all very casual. Emily sat in her high chair, Sam and David Michael sat on the worktops, Karen (for some reason) sat on the floor, and everyone else sat at the table.

I watched Karen eat her dessert. First she knocked the ice cream off the pie. Then she ate the pie filling. Then she ate the crust. Then she stirred the ice cream into vanilla soup. Then she drank her "soup" from the plate. Finally she ran into the bathroom, where apparently she checked herself in the mirror, before charging right back out, crying, "Look at me! I'm ill! I've got a blue tongue. And blue teeth. "I've got the winter blues."

Bart burst out laughing. "That's a good joke!"

I whispered to him, "I'm not sure she knows what she said."

"Well, it's still funny."

We finished our desserts and piled the dishes in the sink. Karen began to prance around the kitchen, singing, "*Oh, the weather outside is frightful. But the fire inside's delightful. Da, da, da, da, da, doe, doe, doe. Let it snow, let it snow, let it snow!* . . . Thank you! Thank you, ladies and gentlemen."

"Oh, wonderful!" I said to Mum. "What a good idea this was. We should be sure to give Karen a load of sugar every night just before her bedtime. Especially when we've got visitors."

Mum smiled at me. "Darling, Bart's got a little brother. I'm sure he's used to the things children do. Just relax."

"Is he used to *that*?" I pointed to Karen, who was wearing her jumper-pants again. She was modelling them for Bart as she sang, "*In the meadow we will build a snowman, and pretend that he is Parson Brown . . .*"

"Well, Karen gets excited about things," said Mum. "You remember how thrilling snow was when you were seven, don't you?"

"Of course," I replied. "I just hope I never danced around in jumper-pants, singing old songs in front of someone's important boyfriend."

Why, I wondered, had I wanted Bart to have a

chance to get to know my family? They were embarrassing me beyond all reason.

Later, Bart and my brothers and Karen and I were watching TV. Watson was putting Emily Michelle to bed. Mum and Nannie were talking in the living room. "Kristy?" said Bart.

"Yes?"

"I should probably go home now. It's getting rather late."

"Okay." I looked out of the window. "Gosh, it's snowing as hard as ever. I wonder if Watson will want to drive yet. Come on. We'll talk to Mum." Bart and I went into the living room. "Mum? Bart says he should be getting home, but it's still snowing really hard," I told her.

"I can walk," Bart offered again.

"I don't know," said Mum.

"I'm going to check outside," I announced. I opened the front door. Then I tried to push open the storm door. "Hey, it's stuck!" I exclaimed. I pushed harder.

Watson appeared behind me and flicked on the porch light.

"Wow!" I cried. "Look at that! No wonder I couldn't open the door." Snow was piled against it, blown there by the wind. "Hey, this is a real storm," I added. "Not just some snow shower . . . How is Bart going to get home? He can't go out in a storm." (I knew Watson wasn't going to haul out his car, even if he *had* just put on its snow tyres.)

"Bart, why don't you spend the night here?" suggested Mum.

Spend the night? What a ridiculously simple solution to the problem. Why hadn't I thought of it? No. Wait. *Bart* spend the night at *my* house with *my* family? Was I on a suicide mission?

"Um, Mum," I said hoarsely, "I don't think that's a very good idea."

Unfortunately, Bart answered my mother at the same time. "Oh, thanks, Mrs Brewer. That would be wonderful. I'll ring my parents."

I was torn. I didn't know whether to follow Bart to the kitchen or stay behind to question my mother's sanity. Finally, I just mouthed "ARE YOU CRAZY?" to Mum, then followed Bart.

In the kitchen, Bart picked up the phone, dialled his number, and spoke to his dad. "Yes, dinner was great . . . Mm-hmm. . . . Blueberry pie. . . . So, anyway, Kristy's mother said I might as well just spend the night. Is that okay? I'll see you—I'll see you—Dad? Dad?" Bart turned to me. "The line went dead," he reported.

The words had barely left his mouth when everything went dark. I could hear appliances turning off throughout the house. The TV flicked off, a radio flicked off, even the fridge turned itself off.

"Uh-oh! Power cut," I said needlessly.

From the TV room, Andrew shrieked. "Turn on the lights!" he cried.

"Andrew hates the dark," I informed Bart. I found a torch, and we made our way into the study. "The storm must have knocked down the power lines," I said to Andrew. "It'll be okay."

Andrew was hugging my legs and sniffling. Karen looked worried. "I hope the lights come on before Christmas," she said.

And Bart said, "I'm glad I was able to talk to my dad."

Mum and Nannie and Watson joined us in the study with some more torches. "We might as well go to bed now," said Watson.

David Michael snorted. "Where's Bart going to sleep? In Kristy's room?"

"No, Toast-for-Brains," I said. "We'll give him a guest room."

Going to bed had never been more excruiciat-ing. I couldn't, of course, let Bart see me in my pyjamas. This meant I had to wait till everybody had finished using the bathroom. Then I went in, quickly washed my face and brushed my teeth, and darted back to my room. I locked the door behind me before I changed out of my clothes. We aren't supposed to sleep with our doors locked (in case of fire), but I didn't want Bart accidentally sleepwalking into my room during the night or something. I lay awake till nearly one o'clock, trying to work out what to do, and also wondering what my friends had been up to that evening. At 12:53 I finally dared to unlock the door. Then I leapt into bed and huddled under the covers, very aware of the fact that Bart was sleeping just a couple of rooms down the hall.

How was a person supposed to relax under such conditions? And, oh lord! what would happen the next morning when I woke up, bleary-eyed and fuzzy-tongued? I couldn't let Bart see me that way.

I set my alarm for five-thirty.

12th CHAPTER

Claudia

Wednesday Evening

I always have fun when I sit for Mariah
and Gabie and Laura. They are such good kids.
Just like evry other kid in stoneybrook they
were realy exited for the snow. As soon as
the flaks started to fall, Maria began to plan
how to spend Thrusday. "I no I wont have
school" she said. "We can go skating and
billed snow peopul and maybe make hot
choclate." she and gabie were so so happy.
Of course that was befer the lights went out
and the phone stoped working.

My job at the Perkinses' started at six o'clock on Wednesday evening, as soon as I'd finished taking the BSC calls. On my way across the street, I realized it was snowing—just tiny little flakes, but they were better than nothing.

The house the Perkins girls live in, the one opposite mine, is pretty special. Guess why? It used to be Kristy's house. She and her mother and Sam and Charlie and David Michael lived there before Kristy's mum married Watson and the Thomases moved to his mansion. Myriah Perkins, who's five and a half, sleeps in Kristy's old room now. She's got two younger sisters— Gabbie, who's almost three, and Laura, who's a baby. My friends and I love to sit for the Perkinses.

I knew that the girls (well, the older two) would be glad to hear about the snow, so as soon as Myriah and Gabbie opened the door, I said, "Surprise! It's snowing!"

"Great!" Gabbie exclaimed, bouncing onto the porch in her socks.

"Whoa!" I said. "You'll freeze with no shoes on. Come inside with me."

"Mummy and Daddy are going to dinner at the Vansants'," Myriah said as I ushered Gabbie inside. "The Vansants live far, far away in the country. They live on a farm. They've got a *horse!*"

"Cool!" I said.

"Hello, Claudia!" Mrs Perkins greeted me. She sat Laura in her baby bouncer. (It's suspended from the top of a door frame. It's mounted on springs. Laura bounces happily in it every day now.)

"Hi!" I replied. "Hi, Mr Perkins! Hi, Laura! Guess what? It's starting to snow."

"You're kidding!" said Mr Perkins. "Huh! The weatherman was right."

"We'll have to be extra careful on the roads," said Mrs Perkins to her husband.

"Oh, it's just a dusting," I went on. "Nothing much."

The Perkinses gave me instructions for the evening—what to make for dinner, when to put the girls to bed, where to find the Vansants' phone number. "We'll be home before ten," added Mr Perkins.

"Okay, you lot. Who's hungry?" I said when Mr and Mrs Perkins had left.

"Me!" said Myriah.

"I want Mummy," said Gabbie.

"She'll be here when you wake up tomorrow," I assured her. "And I'll tell her to kiss you goodnight when she comes home. Is that okay?"

Gabbie nodded.

"I'd like her to kiss me, too," said Myriah politely.

"Okay. Now—I'm going to get supper ready. Laura can bounce in her chair. Myriah, why don't

you and Gabbie keep a watch on the snow for me?
You can give me a weather report at dinner. The
living room window can be the Weather Centre,
like on the news."

"Yes!" exclaimed Myriah. "Gabbie, come on.
We've got an important job to do."

Mrs Perkins had told me that a pot of leftover
spaghetti was in the fridge. I heated that up in the
double boiler while I prepared a salad. Then I got
out Laura's baby food.

"Dinner!" I called.

Myriah and Gabbie came running. As I lifted
Laura out of her bouncer and put her in her high
chair, Myriah announced, "We've got a weather
report for you. Outside, it's very, very cold. We
think the wind's starting to blow. And the
snowflakes are bigger now."

"There's snow all over the grass," added
Gabbie. "Everywhere."

Maybe I should have paid more attention to the
girls' report. But I didn't. I was too busy serving
spaghetti, feeding Laura, and trying to feed
myself. Then, in the middle of all *that*, Myriah
said, "I think the pets are hungry."

"The pets!" I cried. I had forgotten to feed
them. Mrs Perkins had said to put their food out
while we were eating dinner.

The pets are Chewbacca, a wonderful, lovable,
but slightly crazy black Labrador retriever; a cat,
R.C., which stands for Ratcatcher; and a new

101

kitten, Socks Sebastian Perkins, known as Socks. (His fur's orange everywhere except on his feet, which are white, so he looks as if he's wearing two pairs of socks.)

I filled Chewbacca's dish with yucky dog food, and the cats' dishes with Kibbles. Then I gave them fresh water.

"Okay, Laura. Now you can eat," I said, holding a spoonful of mashed carrots towards her mouth.

Laura opened her mouth obediently. She took the carrot goo—but she didn't swallow it. She smiled, then laughed, and the next thing I knew, I was wearing carrots across my front. Luckily, I'd prepared myself for this possibility. I've fed enough babies to know that they shouldn't be the only ones wearing bibs.

I'm so, so happy it's snowing!" said Myriah from the end of the table. "I don't think I'll have to go to kindergarten tomorrow."

"Don't you like kindergarten?" Gabbie asked her sister.

"Yes," replied Myriah. "I do. It's fun. But tomorrow the snow will be even more fun. We can go sledging in the back garden."

"And make a snowman!" added Gabbie.

"Or a whole snow family!" cried Myriah. "A snow mummy and a snow daddy and three snow girls and a snow dog and two snow cats."

"You're going to be very busy tomorrow," I said.

"That's what happens when you're five," Myriah replied.

Myriah and Gabbie finished their supper and ate apples for dessert. Laura gobbled up her carrots and some beef baby food and drank some milk.

"Listen, you two," I said to Myriah and Gabbie. "I'm going to put Laura to bed in a few minutes. Can you play upstairs till I've finished? Then I'll come downstairs with you."

I carried Laura up to her room. I was followed by Myriah and Gabbie, who came into Gabbie's room to look at picture books.

"Okay, Laura-Lou," I said. I laid her in her cot and took off her blue overalls. I changed her nappy. Then I slipped her into a fluffy yellow suit. Finally, I switched on her music box and night-light, and turned off the lamp on her chest of drawers. "Sleep tight," I said, rubbing her back. I tiptoed out of the room.

From down the hall I could hear Myriah chanting, "Run, run as fast as you can!" And Gabbie chiming in with, "You can't catch me, I'm the Gingerbread Man!"

The girls kept me busy that evening. They had invented a game they wanted me to play with them. They decided they needed milk and biscuits. They wanted to watch a TV programme, which I couldn't seem to find, no matter how many times I flipped through the channels. They played a noisy game of tag with Socks, who kept running into small places where he couldn't be reached.

Finally, I had to announce, "Bedtime!" I knew this wouldn't be greeted with cheers or squeals of delight. However, I was somewhat surprised when, instead of "Do we *have* to, Claudia?" I heard *ring, ring*!

"Telephone!" cried Gabbie. "Can I get it?"

"I think I'd better," I answered. "But you can say hello." I picked up the receiver. "Hello, Perkins residence. This is Claudia."

"Hi, Claudia! It's Mr Perkins."

"Oh! Hi! Is everything all right?"

"Technically, yes. But . . . Mrs Perkins and I aren't going to be able to come home tonight. The roads are *awful*. They're slippery, and most of them haven't been cleared. We left early, but we had to turn round and come back."

"Wow!" I exclaimed. "I didn't think the snow was that bad."

"Neither did we, till we tried to drive in it. We're at the Vansants' house now, and we're going to spend the night here. Do you think you could stay with the girls? I know it's asking a lot. Or maybe you could take them over to your house. Are your parents at home?"

"Yup. Don't worry about anything. I'll work this out. The girls will be fine."

I let both Gabbie and Myriah talk to their parents for a few moments. When they'd finished, I rang my own parents and told them what had happened.

"I'll be right over," said my mother.

"Oh, you don't have to come. Honestly. It's awful outside. We'll be all right. And if anything does happen I can just phone you or come over. Okay?"

"Okay," agreed Mum.

We rang off. I could hardly contain my excitement. What an adventure this was! Babysitting by myself, overnight, for three children including a baby. I would have quite a story to tell my BSC friends. Suddenly, I felt like phoning them. We could talk for a few minutes and catch up with each others' news. I wanted to find out how Stacey's perm looked, whether Dawn was back from the airport . . .

"Claudia?" said a little voice. It was Gabbie. I stopped daydreaming and looked down at her. "Mummy isn't going to kiss me goodnight tonight. You said she would, but she isn't coming home."

"Oh, Gabbers. I'm sorry," I replied. "I didn't realize we were having a big snowstorm. But do you know what? Your mummy and daddy will be home tomorrow" (I hoped) "and they can both

105

kiss you then. So I think you two should say goodnight to Socks and R.C. and Chewy now. It's almost bedtime."

"Okay," agreed Gabbie, looking tearful but brave.

Myriah and Gabbie found the cats. They said goodnight to them, and kissed their tails. Then they went off in search of Chewbacca.

You'd think a large, noisy dog would be easy to find. But the girls looked in Chewy's favourite spots and couldn't see any sign of him.

"I bet he's in the laundry room," said Myriah. No Chewy.

"Maybe he's under the big table," said Gabbie. "He often sleeps there."

We looked under the dining room table. No Chewy.

"Okay, we'll search the house," I announced.

The girls and I looked through every room. We looked in tiny places where Chewbacca couldn't possibly fit. Gabbie even looked in Laura's cot. No Chewy. We called and whistled and whistled and called.

"Chewy's missing!" Myriah announced tearfully.

"Calm down," I said to the girls. "I'll phone Mum and Dad. They'll know what to do. They can come over and help us."

I reached for the phone, started to dial our

number, and realized the phone was dead. No dialling tone. "Uh-oh!" I said.

I hung up the useless phone . . . just as the power cut out and the girls and I found ourselves in darkness.

13th CHAPTER

Jessi

Wednesday Evening

I spent the night at my ballet school. That was pretty unusual. Spending the night at any school is unusual, I suppose; but I was stuck at dance school with a group of teachers and kids I didn't know terribly well.

A lot of the little kids were scared. Their sense of time

is different from older kids' or from adults'. If you say, "You'll see your dad and mum tomorrow," they understand the concept (you know, like, you'll see them "later"), but "later" could be in a day or a decade.

Plus, I was worried about Quint, but as it turned out, I didn't need to be.

Not a single parent turned up that night. Not one.

The phone never stopped ringing, though.

People kept ringing and ringing. "We just can't make it," they'd say. "The storm took us by surprise. I don't know what to do."

The teachers told them not to worry. "All the children are here," they'd say. "And we're happy to stay with them. There's food in the kitchen. We'll be fine till tomorrow."

I can't say that I'd been hoping for an adventure, but I seemed to have found one. Personally, I thought Quint's visit would be enough of an adventure. But now I was going to

109

be staying at school, sleeping on my coat and eating Lipton's Cup-O-Noodles soup.

I would be warm, dry, and full—which was more than I could say about Quint. I didn't even know where he *was*.

"Worrying doesn't help anything," Mama always says.

But the more I thought about Quint, the more worries I invented.

What was he doing? Freezing at the railway station? Looking around frantically for my father? Maybe he'd phoned my house—if he'd brought our number with him, and if he had the right change. That would be the sensible thing to do. In fact, it was what *I* should do.

However, I wasn't the only person who wanted to use the phone in the school office. I joined a queue of about eight children who were waiting to make calls. The little girl in front of me, who was about seven years old, was crying quietly. So quietly, in fact, that the teachers hadn't noticed she was crying. Their hands were full taking care of the children who were crying noisily.

"Hey, what's the matter?" I asked the girl. She shook her head. A large tear trickled down her cheek. "Are you Holly?" I asked, groping for the name I thought I remembered Mme Noelle using earlier.

"Yes," Holly said, sniffling.

110

Jessi

"You're Jessi, aren't you?"

"Yes. Why are you crying?"

Holly's lower lip trembled. "Because I don't want to spend the night here. I want my mummy and daddy. And Christopher. And Tattoo. He's our collie dog. And Caboose, my baby doll."

"Your doll's name is Caboose?"

"Yes. And I always sleep with Caboose. Every night."

"But we're going to have a sleepover adventure here at school."

"I don't want to sleep here. I've never slept here before."

"Pretend it's a hotel."

"I've never slept in a hotel, either."

"Have you ever slept away from home?" I asked.

"No," said Holly with a sob.

Uh-oh! This was a tricky situation. I took Holly's hand and squeezed it. Then I held onto it. "I'll stay with you till you talk to your parents, okay? You can pretend I'm your . . ." Hmm. Her what?

"My big sister?" Holly suggested.

"Right!" I grinned. "Your big sister."

The queue for the phone was moving at a snail's pace. A sleepy snail. Mme Duprès was overseeing things, and she tried to limit conversations to three minutes, but the little children were scared and didn't want to say goodbye to their parents.

At long last, the boy in front of Holly rang off.

111

Holly took the phone. She had to dial her number with her left hand, since her right hand was occupied holding onto *my* hand.

"Hi, Mummy?" Holly said, and burst into tears.

I felt sorry for Holly's mother. How awful to get a call from a crying child and not be able to "make it all better".

"*Please* come and get me," Holly kept begging.

After three minutes, Mme Duprès tapped Holly gently on the shoulder. Holly managed to ring off. She looked at me. "Mummy and Daddy can't come. The roads are too dangerous. That's what they said."

I nodded. "I'm sorry, Holly. Hey, do you want to stay with me while I phone *my* parents? I might need you."

"Okay." Holly kept a grip on my hand.

I dialled home. *Buzz-buzz-buzz*. Bother! The phone was engaged. I glanced at the queue of children behind me, still waiting to phone their families. "Can I try once more?" I asked Mme Duprès. "It was engaged."

She gave me permission, and I dialled again. Still engaged.

"Okay, thanks," I mumbled. I left the office, Holly still attached to me.

Until then, I'd been able to convince myself that Quint would ring my parents, find out Daddy couldn't pick him up, and then . . .? Then

112

what? I asked myself. Would Quint turn round and go home? (If the trains were still running.) Surely, Quint had phoned his own parents. That was it! I should phone Quint's family in New York.

But what if they *hadn't* heard from him? What if they were assuming Daddy had picked up Quint and me as planned, and we were all safe at home, enjoying the blizzard from our fireside? I didn't want to worry them. But *I* was worried. *I* needed to know where Quint was and that he was safe.

"Jessi? What are you thinking about?" asked Holly. "You look sad."

"Oh. I'm not sad, really. Just a bit worried."

"Why?"

I explained to Holly, as simply as I could, about Quint and the train and Daddy. "So I'm not sure where Quint is," I finished up. "I mean, he's probably at the station, but I'm not sure."

"Why don't you ring the station?" asked Holly. "Maybe somebody could go, 'Quint, Quint!' over the loudspeaker. They could say, 'You've got a call from Jessi. Please go to a red circus phone,' or whatever it's called."

"Courtesy phone," I supplied. "Hey, that's a good idea, Holly. I could ask someone to page Quint for me. Then I could talk to him myself."

But I'd already had a turn on the phone. I would have to wait a while for another.

Holly and I wandered back to the room in which we'd held our rehearsal that afternoon. Two teachers were there, along with a group of the youngest children.

Most of the children were about Holly's age. Several were crying. The teachers were trying to comfort them, but they couldn't deal with all of them at the same time.

I suppose taking care of children comes naturally to me, what with Becca and Squirt and my babysitting jobs. Holly and I approached the nearest sobbing child, a little boy with huge brown eyes.

"Do you know who this is?" I asked Holly.

She nodded. "Yup. That's Gianmarco. He plays a mouse."

"Hi, Gianmarco!" I said. "I'm Jessi. You probably aren't used to seeing me in my ordinary clothes, I play the Mouse King."

"Oh." Gianmarco wouldn't look at me.

"Are you worried about your parents?" I asked.

"My dad." Gianmarco bit his lower lip.

"You know what? My dad couldn't pick me up, either," I told him. "A lot of mums and dads decided not to drive in the snow. Trust me, they're safer at home."

"But what about us?" wailed Gianmarco.

"Yes, what about us?" Holly chimed in.

"We're going to stay right here and have a

wonderful time. It'll be like a big party. Hey, look!" I pointed across the room. "Here comes dinner." The school secretary was struggling through the doorway with a tray of paper cups, plastic spoons, packets of instant soup and dried fruit, and a plate of biscuits left over from a party the teachers had held recently.

"Where are we going to eat?" asked Holly.

"Well, we're going to eat, um," I paused, "right here on the floor. We'll have a picnic. Okay, everyone? Let's find our coats, spread them on the floor, and sit on them. We'll pretend they're one big blanket, and we're having a picnic in the country . . . Mmm, I think I can smell hot dogs!"

"I smell pizza!" cried Gianmarco.

He and Holly and I sat on the floor, eating instant soup and butter biscuits.

"Simply delicious hamburgers!" commented Holly.

"Awesome ice-cream sundae!" added another voice.

One by one the children were joining our imaginary picnic.

Mme Noelle peeped into the room and smiled gratefully at me.

Twenty minutes later, the children were calmer. Some of them seemed to be enjoying the adventure. I decided to try phoning Quint at the railway station.

115

I stood up. "I'll be right back," I said to Holly.

But she wasn't listening to me. She was staring at the doorway to the room. "Who's that?" she whispered.

I turned round. In the doorway stood . . . Quint.

I ran to him and threw my arms round him. He was snow-covered and frozen, but he seemed fine. "How did you get here?" I cried.

"I walked," Quint replied through chattering teeth. "When your dad didn't turn up, I guessed he couldn't drive in the snow. So I asked a man at the railway station for directions to the dance school. And here I am."

I hardly dared to believe what was happening. But after a few moments, I came to my senses. "We must call my parents—and yours—and tell them where you are," I said.

I led Quint into the office. When we picked up the receiver, we discovered the phone had gone dead.

14th CHAPTER

Mary Anne

Wednesday Evening
Our overnight sitting job
turned into even more of
an adventure than Mallory
and I had expected. First
came the snow, then came
the phone call from Mr
and Mrs Pike. Oh, the
Abominable Snowman
caused some excitement, too....

"The Abominable Snowman?" Claire repeated. She gave Adam a long, hard look. "He steals homework? Then, does that mean he comes into houses?"

"Of course," Adam replied. "What did you think? That he steals homework from teachers? That's no fun. He has to steal homework *before* kids hand it in to their teachers. Then he roars at them, 'Do it again!'"

"Does he come into your *room*?" Claire persisted.

"That depends on where your homework is. If it's in your school locker, he goes into your locker. If it's at home, he goes into your bedroom."

I could see Claire forming another question. She was about to ask it when the phone rang. Instead she dived for the phone. "Hi, Mummy!" she exclaimed when she'd answered it. "It's snowing!"

Claire told Mrs Pike how the day had gone. Then she handed the phone to Mallory. "Mummy wants to talk to you," she said.

Mallory took the phone. She listened, her face growing more and more serious. She kept saying. "Mm-hmm, mm-hmm."

"What?" Jordan whispered, elbowing Mallory. "What's Mum saying?"

Mal shrugged him off and turned to face the wall. "Mm-hmm, mm-hmm. . . . Okay, hang on a sec. Mary Anne, Mum wants to talk to you now."

118

"Hi, Mrs Pike!" I said, cradling the receiver between my ear and shoulder.

"Hi, Mary Anne! Listen, it's snowing in New York, too, and the trains have stopped running. We aren't going to be able to get home tonight."

"Wow!" I whispered. "Um, okay. Well, we'll be all right."

"This is a big responsibility," said Mrs Pike.

"I know, but as I said, my dad's at home. And Mrs Barrett. And Mrs McGill."

"Right. Listen, will you and Mallory tell the others that we'll see them tomorrow? Oh, and we're staying with the Sombergs. We gave you their number before we left. Phone if you need to. Otherwise, we'll talk in the morning. I'll phone you when we know what our plans are."

"Okay," I agreed.

We rang off. I was slightly nervous about telling the younger Pike children that their parents wouldn't be home till the next day—but they didn't care.

"We'll be pioneers!" exclaimed Margo. "Snow pioneers."

And Nicky jumped around crying, "No school, no parents! No school, no parents!"

"It's a shame he's so upset about it," Mal whispered to me.

I giggled. "I'd better call my dad," I said then. "He should know what's going on. I'll call Mrs Barrett, too."

119

"Thanks," said Mallory. "I'll try to settle the children down."

"Hello, Dad?" I said a few moments later. "Guess what." I explained the situation to him. I must have sounded awfully calm, because instead of getting hysterical and crying out "I'll be right over!" he just said, "Do you want me to come over, darling?"

"I think we're okay," I replied. "We wouldn't have seen Mr and Mrs Pike until tomorrow, even if they *had* come home on time."

"All right. Just as well. I haven't heard from Sharon and I'd like to be here if she phones. I want to know that she and Dawn reached the airport safely."

"Okay. I'm going to call Mrs Barrett now, just so she knows we're on our own here tonight. I'll talk to you later this evening."

"'Night, darling."

"'Night, Dad."

I called Mrs Barrett as I'd planned. Then I decided to phone Stacey. It wouldn't hurt to let her and her mum know what Mal and I were up to.

I glanced out of the kitchen window. The Pikes' back windows face the McGills' back windows, across their gardens.

Funny, I thought. Stacey's house was dark. Had she and her mum already gone to bed? It wasn't likely. I tried to remember if their lights had been on when Mal and the children and I were playing in the snow, but I couldn't. I hesitated, then dialled Stacey's number, praying I wouldn't wake her or her mother.

Ring, ring, ring, ring . . . The phone eventually rang seven times before I decided no one was going to answer it.

I hung up. "Hey, Mal!" I called.

"Yes?"

I found the children in the playroom, slumped in front of the TV. "Mal, no one's at home at Stacey's. Isn't that odd?"

"A bit. Maybe they got stuck somewhere when the snow came. At a friend's house, perhaps. What was Stacey doing this afternoon?"

"I'm not sure." I tried to picture the appointment pages from the BSC notebook. Had Stacey been scheduled for a babysitting job? I didn't think so.

"Oh, well. Wherever they are, I'm sure they're fine," said Mal.

"Yes."

"Mal?" spoke up Bryon. "I'm hungry."

"But you've just had hot chocolate. And before that, you had dinner."

"I'm still hungry."

"Me, too," said Nicky and Vanessa.

Mal heaved a sigh. "I'll go and see what there is," she said, and disappeared upstairs. "Hey,

Mary Anne! Come here!" she called a minute later.

I ran to the kitchen. "What?" I asked.

"I've just realized something. We've got hardly any food."

"You're kidding!"

"No. Mum left enough for breakfast today and tomorrow, and for tonight's dinner, but then she was going to get in a lot of shopping when she got home tomorrow. She didn't even have stuff for our lunches, remember?"

"But you must have *some* food," I said, frowning.

"Oh, yes. We've got plenty of flour and sugar and coffee and icing mix. And I think I saw a couple of instant meals in the freezer. But we're nearly out of milk, eggs, breakfast cereal, juice, fruit, bread—"

"Okay, I get the picture," I interrupted.

"So what are we going to do tomorrow if Mum and Dad don't get home and we can't leave the house?"

"Well, we won't starve. Trust me. We'll borrow stuff from the Barretts. We'll eat icing if we have to."

"Hey, I've just thought of something!" exclaimed Mal. "How much emergency money did Mum give us?"

"A lot," I replied.

"Enough to order in a couple of pizzas?"

122

"Definitely. If the vans can make deliveries, we're okay. Want to call Pizza Express?"

"As quickly as possible," replied Mallory.

"Okay." I picked up the phone and held it to my ear. I shook the receiver.

"What's wrong?" asked Mal.

"The phone's not working."

"Huh. That's wei— Hey!"

We'd been standing in the kitchen, talking, and now we couldn't see a thing. Not even our hands. The house was in total darkness.

"Help!" yelled Margo from the playroom.

That was followed by the sound of Claire crying.

"The TV's gone off!" shouted Adam.

I thought the house seemed really quiet. Now I knew why. The power was off as well as the phone. *Nothing* was working—not the TV, not the radios, not the fridge, not the stereo.

Mal and I spent the next few minutes calming Claire and Margo, hunting for torches, and trying to remember which appliances had been on so that we could turn them off. We had just switched off the television when a horrible thought occurred to me.

What if the heat didn't work? We could freeze to death.

The heat did work, though. It was practically the only thing that did.

"Thank goodness!" I murmured.

123

Mary anne

Mal, her brothers and sisters, and I crowded on to a couple of sofas in the playroom. We'd found three torches, and they were turned on. Our faces looked ghostly in the dark house.

"Hey, Claire," said Adam. "Did I mention that the Abominable Snowman likes the dark?"

"Yikes!" shrieked Claire.

15th CHAPTER

Dawn

Wednesday Evening
Wednesday night was one of
the longest in my life. Somehow,
it even seemed longer than the
nights when Claud and I were
stranded on that island after
the boat wreck. For one thing,
there's nothing like sleeping in
a hard plastic chair. For another,
there's nothing like sleeping in a
hard plastic chair with about
twenty-five other people who are
doing the same thing.

Guess what Mum and I found when we reached Jeff's gate at the airport?

A smiling and relieved Jeff? No.

An anxious and hysterical Jeff? No.

Pandemonium? Well, almost.

A lot of people were crowded around the ticket desk. An agent from the airline was trying to talk to them, but they were making so much noise they couldn't hear what he was saying.

I glanced at Mum. "This doesn't look good," I said.

Mum strode to the desk and joined the crowd. Since no one would quieten down, the agent gave up trying to speak. He started to leave the desk. *Then* everybody shut up.

The man, looking annoyed, said, "Thank you. As I said a moment ago, the flight from Los Angeles has been delayed. Currently, the scheduled arrival time is about an hour from now. I'll keep you updated periodically and will let you know quickly if there's a change of plan."

"Mum!" I exclaimed. "Jeff isn't here yet!" What a relief. That meant he wasn't wandering around feeling abandoned.

"Right." Mum smiled.

"It's a good thing he doesn't get airsick, though. The plane's probably circling. Imagine circling for an hour!"

My mother made a face. "I was once on a plane that circled for two hours. I thought I'd die!"

"Well . . . what shall we do? We've got an hour to kill," I pointed out.

"There's always food," Mum suggested.

"Yes. But we've just had dinner. Besides, do you really think we'll find healthy food in an airport, the capital of bad sandwiches?"

"You never know," said Mum, smiling again. "Anyway, let's wander round. We'll look in the gift shop and the news-stand."

"Okay."

The terminal was boiling hot, so we took off our coats and carried them to the gift shop. The thing about the gift shop is that nearly every item on sale has the word "Connecticut" written on it. These are racks of Connecticut sweat shirts and T-shirts and anoraks, shelves of Connecticut caps and visors, and display case after display case of Connecticut salt and pepper shakers, spoon rests, snow globes, plaques, car stickers, pencil cases, key chains, fridge magnets, paperweights, pens, piggy banks, plates, mugs—you name it.

"Hey, Mum!" I said. "If your plane landed at this airport and for some reason you weren't sure what state you were in, do you think you could work it out by coming into this shop?"

Mum frowned, and pretended to look all around her. At last she said, "No."

We looked in the news-stand next, which is more like a shop than a stand. And it stocked paperback books, too. I bet you can find a copy of any magazine in the country there. I leafed through a magazine about California. I read an entire article. Then I looked at my watch. Half an hour had gone by.

A cold feeling washed over me.

"Mum!" I said with a gasp. I thrust the magazine back onto the stand. "I've just thought of something."

My mother must have seen the panic in my face. "What?" she exclaimed.

"Jeff's probably going mad on the plane. I was relieved when the man said the plane hadn't landed yet, but Jeff's probably scared anyway. Maybe he's wondering whether we'll wait for him. Also, when he does land, how are we going to get home? It's still snowing."

"Dawn, you're picking up Mary Anne's one bad habit, which is worrying too much. We can't do anything now except wait. I hope Jeff knows we wouldn't turn round and leave the airport without him. And as for the snow, I don't know. Maybe by the time Jeff arrives, it will have let up. I won't do anything foolish."

"I know you won't," I said. "Sorry."

Mum gave me a hug. "You don't have to apologize," she said.

She paid for a copy of *The New York Times*, and we went back to Jeff's gate. We sat in these awful, hard plastic chairs. They were the chairs I mentioned earlier that were so, so uncomfortable.

You know, Claud and I really did get stranded on an island once. Not a desert island, just a small island off the coast of Connecticut. We'd been out sailing, a storm had blown up, one of our boats was wrecked, and we were washed ashore on the island, where we stayed until we were rescued a few days later.

"May I have your attention, please?" The airline official was speaking into a microphone at the ticket desk again. Guess what he announced this time? He announced that Jeff's plane wouldn't be arriving at *all* that night. It had been diverted to Washington, D.C. because of the snow (which apparently Washington wasn't getting).

"Washington?!" I shrieked to my mother. "But Jeff —"

"Hold on a sec," said Mum, cutting me off. "I'll go and talk to the agent. You stay here and watch our coats, please."

I bit my nails as I watched Mum hurry to the desk and try to talk to the man. Needless to say, she wasn't the only one doing that. So several minutes passed before she came back to her seat.

"What did he say?" I asked.

"Just what he said before. The plane can't land because of the snow, so it's being diverted to Washington, which is getting a little rain but nothing else. It can land safely there."

"But how's Jeff going to get *here*?" I cried.

129

"The man said the passengers will be flown to Connecticut tomorrow morning, if the weather has improved and the runway is clear enough."

"Tomorrow! What's Jeff going to do all night?"

"One of the flight attendants will take care of him. Everyone is being put up at a hotel till the morning. The attendant will make sure Jeff gets from the airport to the hotel and back to the airport tomorrow."

Mum sounded much more assured than she looked.

"What do we do now?" I asked.

"Wait around to see if anything changes."

My mother and I sat quietly for a while. Mum tried to read her newspaper, but I don't think she was having any success. She never turned a page. And she jumped a mile when the airline official announced that anyone who needed to do so could make a free phone call to Washington to try to contact the friends or relatives who'd been stranded there.

My mother dashed to the desk. She was the fourth person in the queue to use the telephone. But she never got a chance. The person in front of her was chattering away when suddenly he stopped. Then he said, "Hello? Hello? . . . HELLO?" He turned to the man at the desk. "The phone's gone dead," he informed him.

The man pressed a few buttons, trying to get another line. But it was no use. *All* the phones at the airport were out of order.

130

"Lines must be down," someone said.

"They *can't* be," I replied.

"Attention, please," began a voice, speaking over the paging system. "Unfortunately, I must tell you that the airport is now being closed due to the storm. There will be no more incoming or outgoing flights until further notice. We advise you not to leave the airport to drive anywhere. If you have any questions, please ask someone connected with your airline. Thank you."

"Mum! We're *stuck* here," I exclaimed.

"I know. And now I can't call Richard to let him know where we are. I hope the airport closing gets on the news, and he works out what must have happened and assumes we're safe."

I felt the way I did when Claud and I had been stranded on the island. We'd had to make the best of things then, hoping that soon we'd be with the people we love and that their worrying would be over. So Mum and I settled down for a night at the airport. As it was still fairly early, we went first to the snack bar, which was going to stay open all night, serving food—and free coffee and soft drinks. We discovered that the capital of bad sandwiches sold surprisingly good salads. After we'd eaten, we went to the news-stand. Mum bought us each a book, which we took back to the waiting room. Then we tried to get comfortable in those chairs. This just wasn't possible. We couldn't stretch out. Every time I moved, my

131

spine collided with the armrest or the back or something. Finally I curled into a ball, rested my head on my coat, and tried to read.

16th CHAPTER

Stacey

Wednesday Evening

I'm not sure when I've been more scared. I mean, I really can't think of anything worse than that moment when Mum and I realized we were stuck in the snow and dark in the. middle of who knows where, and would probably be there all night. What about the heat? I worried. If it stopped working, could we freeze to death in a few hours? How fast did that happen? Could we get frostbite and lose our fingers and toes?

Those were the things I was worrying about. Mum was worrying about something else: my diabetes.

At first, the thought that we were in great danger was so stunning that Mum and I couldn't even talk to each other. We sat stiffly in our seats. Mum left the car running so the heater and the headlights could stay on. I tried desperately to work out where we were and then realized it didn't matter. Unless we were *positive* we were near a house or some sort of shelter, it would be foolish to try to walk anywhere.

I gazed out of the window. The sky continued to fling handfuls of snow onto our car. It wasn't even pretty. It was wild and angry and unreasonable.

Mum turned in her seat and sighed, the first sound either of us had made in more than ten minutes. "I'm sorry, darling," she said.

"Hey, this isn't your fault," I replied. But then I couldn't help adding, "Mum, what happens if the heater stops working?"

"We'll stay as close together as we can. For body heat."

"But can you freeze to death overnight?"

"I don't know. I suppose so."

After a long silence I said, "Um, I hate to say this, but I'm hungry."

Mum clapped her hand to her forehead. "What on earth was I thinking of?" she exclaimed. "You need to eat. And your insulin. Have you got—"

"My injection kit is with me," I told her. "I never go anywhere without it.

134

But tonight will be the first time I've had to use it because of a real emergency."

"What about food?" Mum insisted.

"Well, there's the rest of the snack I brought— some carrot sticks and crackers—but I don't know how long that will keep me going. Have you got *any* food with you, Mum?"

"Mints. That's all."

I ate the carrots and crackers.

"Feel better?" Mum asked.

"Sort of," I replied. "But I should be eating dinner now. I need it."

"I know." Mum put her hand on the horn and nearly blasted my head off with the sound.

"Mum! Stop!" I yelled.

"I'm trying to attract attention," she replied, pausing for a moment. "If any houses are around here, maybe someone will hear us."

"And arrest you for disturbing the peace?"

Finally I got a smile out of Mum. "Prison would be warmer than our car," she said. "And I bet there's coffee in prison."

"Mum? What made you fall in love with Dad?" I asked suddenly. The question took me as much by surprise as it took my mother.

"Stace! What a time to ask that," said Mum.

"I want to know."

"Right this second?"

"Have you got anything better to do?"

"I suppose not."

135

"So?"

Mum looked thoughtful. "What makes anyone fall in love with anyone else?" was her response. She spread her hands in her lap, and I noticed that she no longer wore her wedding ring. When had she taken it off?

I waited for Mum to answer her own question, since *I* didn't have an answer. When she didn't I said, "I give up. What?"

Mum shook her head, smiling. "That was a rhetorical question, Stace. It didn't require an answer."

"*My* question wasn't rhetorical. I'm serious. I'm only thirteen. I haven't fallen in love yet. And I want to know what made you fall in love with Dad. This could be an important piece of information."

"Okay. Let me see." Mum paused. "Well," she began, "the first time I can remember thinking I was in love was when I realized your father and I had so many common likes and dislikes that it was as if one of us had been cloned from the other. It seemed that every day we'd discover something new. Not only did we both love the old *I Love Lucy* show, but we shared the same favourite episode."

I giggled. "What else, Mum?"

"Oh, other silly things. Our favourite brand of jeans was Levi's. Our favourite kind of music was swing. Our favourite bandleader was Tommy

136

Dorsey. And we couldn't stand cigarettes. Neither of us had ever smoked one. . . . Darling? What's the matter? Oh, I *told* you this was going to be hard to explain."

"What? It's not that, Mum. Honest. Believe it or not, you were making sense."

"Thanks a lot!"

"You know what I mean. Anyway, it's just that, um, I don't think the heat's on any more. I can't feel it coming out of the vents."

Mum took off one of her gloves and held her bare hand first to one vent, then to another. She fiddled with the control for the heat and tested the vents again. "You're right," she said at last. It isn't working." My mother sank back, resting her head against the seat cushion.

"I think we'll be warm for a while," I said, trying to sound positive. "The heat has *been* on ever since we left the arcade."

Mum sat forward suddenly and rammed her hand on the horn again. The sound blasted through the darkness. She stopped after a few seconds, opened her window a crack, and yelled outside, "HELP! HELP!"

I joined her with a long wail out of my side of the car. 'HE-E-E-E-E-E-LP!"

Honk, honk, ho-o-o-o-onk!

"Help, help, he-e-e-e-e-lp!"

Of course, nothing happened. Who did we think was going to answer us? The trees?

137

When we'd calmed down, Mum said, "I think I'll try to move the car again."

"Are you sure you should open the door and go outside? You'll let cold air in," I told her.

"I don't know," replied Mum, and then she burst into laughter.

"What's so funny?"

"We're out of petrol," she said, giggling helplessly. "I've just noticed. I looked at the petrol gauge. It's on Empty. I don't think we'll be going anywhere tonight." Mum dabbed tears from her eyes.

"That's hysterical?" I said. And then it occurred to me that *Mum* might be hysterical. "Well, tomorrow we'll leave the car and walk till we find help," I said sensibly. "I bet the storm will be over by then. We'll just walk back to the motorway and find a petrol station or a restaurant or something."

"Right."

"I think I'll try to go to sleep," I said. I didn't know what else to do. I couldn't stand watching my mother any more, though.

I closed my eyes.

"Hey!" cried Mum.

"What?" I snapped. I wanted her to leave me alone.

"Someone's coming!" Mum was looking in the rearview mirror. "I can see headlights behind us." Mum leaned on the horn. She blinked our own headlights on and off. And several moments later, an estate car eased to a stop next to our car. A man got out and walked round to Mum's window.

"Mum! You've got no idea who he is!" I cried. "He could be a desperate criminal! I feel as though we're in one of those horror stories they tell at overnight camp. For all you know, he's just escaped from prison."

Mum rolled down her window.

"Do you need some help?" asked the man.

"We certainly do," replied Mum. "We're stuck. We're out of petrol and our heater isn't working. I don't even know where we are."

"My wife and I live just down the road," said the man. "You're welcome to spend the night with us."

Mum turned to me with raised eyebrows.

17th CHAPTER

Mallory

Wednesday Night
and Thursday Morning

I said I was looking forward to a babysitting adventure, but this was a little more than I had had in mind. Now I understand what my father means when he says, "Be careful what you wish for. You might get it." We got an adventure all right -- a blizzard, a power failure, the phone lines down, a food semi-emergency, and an unexpected late-night visitor.

"That's enough about the Abominable Snowman, Adam," I said. "And I mean it. Claire, there's no such thing as an Abominable Snowman."

"Are you sure?" she asked. She was sitting in my lap, holding a torch in one hand. The thumb from her other hand was in her mouth. She was talking round it. *And* playing with her hair. I've never seen a five-year-old do so many things at the same time.

"Positive," I replied.

"I'm still hungry," said Byron.

"I'm scared," said Margo.

"I'm tired of sitting here," said Jordan.

"Let's sing a song," said Claire, whose thumb was still in her mouth. "We sang a good one at school today." She belted out, *Head, shoulders, knees and toes, knees and toes. Head, shoulders, knees and toes, knees and toes. Eyes and ears and nose and mouth and chin. Head, shoulders, knees and toes, knees and toes.*" As Claire mentioned each part of her body, she pointed to it with the torch. Then she cried, "Everybody!"

Mary Anne, Margo, and I joined in. We sang one more chorus. When we paused, Byron said, "My tummy's rumbling."

"We've got to save our food," I informed him.

"How can we?" he replied. "The electricity's off. Everything in the fridge and the freezer is going to spoil."

141

Uh-oh! Mary Anne and I hadn't thought of that.

"I know!" Bryon went on. "We can have a picnic! We'll eat up all the things that will melt or go bad. We'd better start with the ice cream."

"Actually," said Mary Anne, "that isn't a bad idea. We don't know when the power will come back on. If it's off all night, a lot of food *will* get spoiled. We might as well eat some of it."

Vanessa looked wary. "There are frozen vegetables in the freezer," she said hesitatingly. "We haven't got to eat those, have we?" And then she added, "Carrots and sweetcorn and broccoli and beans, you must know that to me this means, um, this means—"

"It means we won't eat most of the stuff in the freezer," supplied Jordan. "Come on, all of you! Forget the vegetables. Let's find the ice cream!"

My brothers and sisters thundered upstairs, guided by their torches. Nicky opened the freezer and Adam pulled out two half-eaten containers of ice cream. "Mint chocolate chip and butter pecan. Let's start with these," he said.

Vanessa shone a torch into the freezer. "There are the vegetables," she said. "I'll just stick them in the back."

Byron, Adam, Jordan, Vanessa, Nicky, Margo, and Claire crowded round the table with spoons and dug into the containers, not bothering with bowls.

"You'd think they'd been brought up by wolves," I whispered to Mary Anne.

She smiled. Then she said, "You know, since we can't get hold of Pizza Express, which probably isn't delivering anyway, and as long as the children are eating, perhaps you and I ought to look around and gather up any food that *won't* go bad. We should say it's off-limits till tomorrow."

"Good idea," I agreed.

While the kids stuffed themselves, Mary Anne and I collected half-empty boxes of cereal, the ends of loaves of bread, several apples, and so on. I was rummaging through a cupboard where I thought Mum had left a box of crackers when . . .

. . . the doorbell rang.

"It's the Abominable Snowman!" shrieked Claire.

"Is it really?" Adam shrieked back. Then he stopped himself. "The Abominable Snowman doesn't bother with doorbells," he said.

"Do robbers?" asked Vanessa.

"I don't think so," I answered uncertainly.

"But who could be out in this weather?" asked Mary Anne. "And at this hour? It's getting rather late."

"Should we answer the door?" asked Nicky, hopping from one foot to the other.

"Someone might need help," I pointed out.

"You lot stay in the kitchen," Mary Anne said

to my brothers and sisters. "Mal and I will see who's at the door."

Mary Anne and I tiptoed through the front hallway. We peered out of the small windows by the door. "I can't make out anything," I said.

"Wait a second, I can see," said Mary Anne. (She only wears glasses for reading. I have to wear them all the time. My vision is about as good as a mole's. Even when my glasses are on.) "It's my dad!" Mary Anne exclaimed.

"Your dad? Are you positive?"

"Yup." Mary Anne opened the door.

Sure enough, standing on the doorstep was her father. "I hope I didn't scare you," he said.

"Oh, no," I replied. (My heart was tap dancing in my chest.)

"I just wanted to make sure you're all right. I was a bit nervous when the lights went out and I couldn't phone you."

"We're fine, Dad," said Mary Anne. "Honestly." She told him what my brothers and sisters were doing. "We're going to go to bed soon," she added.

"All right. I'd offer to stay with you, but Sharon isn't back yet and I didn't hear from her before the phones went, so I'm a bit worried. But I suppose no news is good news."

"Gosh!" I said as Mr Spier stepped carefully down our icy front steps. "Your mum and Dawn aren't back yet, and we don't know where Stacey and *her* mum are. It's rather spooky, isn't it? I wonder what our other friends are doing."

"I wish I knew," replied Mary Anne.

An hour later, Mary Anne and I had succeeded in putting my brothers and sisters to bed. It was quite late—long past their bedtime—but I didn't care. We wouldn't have school the next day, so we could sleep in.

I lay cosily in my warm bed that night. Even so, I didn't sleep much. Probably the sugar from the ice cream and hot chocolate. Also, I couldn't help worrying about Stacey and Dawn. I was going crazy at the thought that I couldn't phone them, or anyone else. Had Jessi and Quint made it back from Stoneybrook or were they stuck somewhere? Was Quint even in Connecticut?

I listened to the wind whistle round the eaves of the house.

Twice, I tiptoed to the window and peeped outside. Not a light anywhere. Not even a street-light. The power hadn't been turned on. I squinted my eyes and tried to see what the blizzard was doing. I was pretty sure snow was still falling, because the snow plough hadn't come down our street yet.

At about two o'clock I fell asleep. But I woke up again before six. I peeped out of the window. Day was breaking, so I could finally see. It was snowing, but only lightly, and I thought the sky

looked brighter than it had on Wednesday afternoon. I tried to guess how much snow had fallen
and decided at least sixty centimetres. Cars were
half buried, our front steps were a small hill of
snow (Mr Spier's footprints had vanished), and
the shrubbery was completely buried.

I wondered if the power was back on yet, and I
turned on the radio alarm clock. A newscaster was
saying, "All state schools, private schools and
church schools are *closed* today."

Yes! No school—and the electricity was back
on.

I switched off the clock before the radio could
wake Mary Anne or Vanessa. Then I tiptoed
downstairs and double-checked the appliances.
The only thing we'd forgotten to switch off was a
light in the playroom, so I turned it off, then
tiptoed back upstairs and checked the boys and
Claire and Margo. They were sleeping peacefully.

I went back to my own bed.

"Mal?" mumbled Mary Anne from her camp
bed.

"Yeah?"

"What's going on?"

"I think the storm's over. Oh, and school's
closed."

18th CHAPTER

Claudia

Wednesday night and
Thursday morning

Waht an evning. Chewy was missing and
the phones werent working and the electricy
was out. I was'nt sure which was the whorst.
Of corse, Chewy's disappearance was awful.
But I needed the phone to call for help. And
electricty would have been nice while I was
searching for him. Iry finding a black dog in
the pitch dark! But I did my best that night
and by the nest day I felt pretty prowd
of myself.

"Hey! Who turned out the lights?" called Myriah.

"Yes, who turned them out?" echoed Gabbie.

"Nobody," I replied.

"Mr Nobody?!" yelped Gabbie.

"No. I mean, nobody turned them out. I think the snow's knocked down some power lines. We probably haven't got any electricity at all. Myriah, do you know where your mum and dad keep their torch?"

"Yes. It's in the cupboard in the playroom. And it's *big*. It needs lots of batteries."

We felt our way through the hall and into the playroom. "Which cupboard?" I asked Myriah. (She and Gabbie were holding onto me by my belt loops.)

"This one, I think," she replied.

I opened the cupboard and reached one hand inside. Since I couldn't see a *thing*, I suddenly became afraid of all sorts of awful creatures that might be hiding there, just waiting for my hand to appear . . . then *snap*! But the first object I touched felt like a torch, so I took it out of the cupboard, fumbled for the switch, found it, pressed it up, and—

Okay. We had light. Now what?

"*There* you are!" exclaimed Gabbie. "And there's Myriah, and here I am!" She sounded amazed.

Okay. We had light. Now what? Put the girls to bed? Carry on with my search for Chewy?

I decided the girls were my first priority, so I guided them carefully upstairs to their bedrooms. They didn't like getting ready for bed in the dark, and I couldn't blame them.

"This is scary," whispered Gabbie.

She was right.

"I don't like walking round corners," said Myriah.

Neither did I.

Nevertheless, I thought I was actually going to get the girls to sleep without problems, until Myriah said, "What if we have to get up during the night? We won't be able to see. Even the night-light in the bathroom doesn't work."

Uh-oh. Good point.

"Well, I need the torch for a little while longer. Until I go to bed," I said. "Then I could put it in the hall or the bathroom and leave it on. How would that be?" I asked, already praying that the batteries wouldn't run out.

"Okay," said Myriah. "Thank you."

"Okay, thank you," said Gabbie.

"Into bed, then," I told the girls. "You're up rather late tonight."

"I've never been to bed in the dark before," said Gabbie.

"Hmm. Why don't you pretend you're going to bed and the light's on as usual?" I suggested. (Gabbie climbed into her bed.) "Now close your eyes," I said. (Gabbie closed them.) "Now open

149

them." (Gabbie opened them.) "See? I've just turned off the light!"

Gabbie giggled.

"Okay." I led Myriah into her room and put her to bed. "I'll be back upstairs in a while," I said. "I'm going to sleep in your room, remember? In the other bed? And I'll put the torch in the hall first."

Myriah smiled. (Or at least I think she did.) As I left her room, she called after me in a loud whisper, "Good luck with Chewy!"

Now how did she know I was going to carry on looking for him?

"Thanks," I replied.

I carried the heavy torch down the steps to the first floor. Once again, I walked from room to room, softly calling, "Chewy! Chewy! Here, boy! Chewy, where are you?" And once again I found nothing. Well , not *nothing*. I found a cat toy under the sofa and a mitten behind a door. In the front hall, I found a letter that had fallen behind a table.

And then I heard footsteps.

I heard footsteps *outside*, padding closer and closer to the—

Ding-dong!

"Oh, my lord!" I shrieked.

"Darling?" called a muffled voice from the other side of the door. "Is that you, Claudia? It's Mum."

150

"Mum?" I called back. "Really?"

"Really. I just wanted to find out if everything was okay."

I opened the door and let her inside. "Mum!" I cried, as if I hadn't seen her for a couple of years. "I'm so glad it's you!"

"Are you all right? Did you know the phones are out of order too? I thought you might have been trying to ring us. Are the girls okay?"

So many questions. I smiled, and my heart, which felt as if it had been beating fast as a hummingbird's slowed down a little. "Yes. We're fine. The girls are asleep. And I did know the phones went off because I tried to call you. Mum, Chewy's missing!"

"Oh, darling. When did you realize he was gone?"

"A little while ago. Myriah and Gabbie wanted to say goodnight to him, and we couldn't find him. I knew he'd been inside before, because I gave him his dinner. And I'm pretty sure no one let him out, but we've looked everywhere. What if he *is* outside? What if he's caught in this storm somewhere? If he doesn't come back, I'll never forgive myself. Poor Chewy. He must be *freezing*."

"Claudia, calm down," said Mum. "I'll help you look through the house again and then we'll call for him outside. That's all we can do. It's much too cold and windy to search outside, and besides, you can hardly see through the snow. If

151

we can't find Chewy tonight, I think you'll have to wait till tomorrow to look any further."

That made sense. "Okay," I agreed.

So Mum and I looked and looked, then leaned out of the front and back doors and called and called. No Chewy.

"I'll stay with you tonight," said Mum as we sank onto the sofa in the playroom. "I can sleep right here."

"Oh, that's okay. Really," I told her. "This job is my responsibility. I don't want anyone to think I can't handle it. And if I do need you, you're right opposite."

"I imagine that by the time we wake up tomorrow, the power will be on again," said my mother. "Maybe the phones will work, too. You'll feel better then. But I *am* happy to stay here."

"No. Thanks, though. I'll ring you first thing in the morning—or I'll bring the girls over for a visit if the phone still doesn't work."

"All right."

Mum left then, and not long afterwards, I went to bed and fell fast asleep. But I didn't stay asleep. I kept waking up, wondering what had happened to Chewy. Sometimes I listened for Laura. I wasn't used to being in charge of a baby for so long. But the Perkinses' house remained quiet till just after five o'clock.

That was when I realized that somebody was

staring at me. From about five centimetres away. I was face-to-face with . . . Gabbie.

"Gabbers?" I whispered. "What are you doing up? Are you okay?"

"I can hear funny sounds, Claudia," she replied.

"Why don't you sleep in here with Myriah and me for a while?"

"No. I want to see what the funny sounds are."

I yawned. "Okay." I said, sitting up. "What do the sounds sound like?"

"I don't know."

Gabbie led me to the top of the stairs. I listened. Sure enough, I could hear funny sounds too. I heard a sort of snuffling and scratching.

"Gabbie!" I exclaimed. "I think it's Chewy!"

I grabbed the torch and we hurried downstairs. We followed the sounds to the basement door. When I opened it, out bounded Chewy.

"Chewbacca!" cried Gabbie.

"Chewy! Have you been in the basement all night? How did you get shut in there anyway? And why didn't you answer us when we called?" (What a question to ask a dog.) "I bet you've got to go to the toilet, haven't you?" I asked, as Gabbie hugged Chewy tightly. I threw my coat on over my nightdress, and let Chewy out of the back door. I didn't follow him, though. I found myself staring at an amazingly white, fuzzy world. Snow was just about all I could see. It had blown and drifted against everything. I had never seen so much snow.

"It's taller than me!" said Gabbie.

It wasn't, but it must have looked that way to her. Anyway, it was more than half as tall as she was.

When Chewy came back inside, I dried him off. I looked at my watch. Not even five-thirty. But the girls and I were up for the day. Laura woke up because she needed a clean nappy.

Myriah woke up because Chewy ran to her bedroom and gave her sloppy kisses.

We checked the electricity. Working! We checked the phone. Working! We listened to the radio. School was closed!

After I'd called Mum, I had fun helping the girls get dressed and then making breakfast for them. In the middle of our breakfast, Mr Perkins phoned, saying that he and Mrs Perkins would be home as soon as the roads had been cleared.

"Would you like dessert?" I asked Myriah and Gabbie later.

"Dessert after breakfast?" said Myriah.

"Yes. We've just had a blizzard. We should make snow cream straight away." I showed the girls how to collect clean snow and put a scoop into a bowl. Then I poured maple syrup over each scoop.

"Yummy!" said Myriah.

"Yummy!" said Gabbie.

And soon they were off outdoors to begin making their snow family.

19th CHAPTER

Jessi

Wednesday Night
and Thursday Morning

I was really
proud of Holly and
the other young kids
who spent the night
at our dance school.
They were quite calm,
all things considered.
I'm not sure I
would have handled
myself that well
when I was their
age. Of course, this
doesn't mean there
was no complaining.
There was whining

*and complaining, but
mostly, I think the
kids had fun. And
so did I!*

By about nine o'clock on Wednesday night, the younger dance students started to get tired. They quarrelled with each other. They spilled things. They whined.

"Sounds like bedtime," I whispered to Quint.

"You're right," Quint replied.

"Somehow, I'd thought we might be home by now," I went on. "I kept thinking the storm would stop suddenly, the snow ploughs would get through, and our parents would arrive. I suppose not." I was looking out of the window. If anything, the snow was coming down even harder.

Quint shook his head. "We're here for the night."

At least the electricity was on. I didn't know that Stoneybrook was without power, so I didn't realize how lucky I was to be stranded in Stamford. All I could see were the problems, though I tried not to dwell on them. The business with the phones was particularly upsetting. I was sure that from New York City to Stoneybrook there was a trail of worried people, especially families. As far as I knew, Quint's parents weren't sure where their son was. *My* parents weren't sure where Quint was. They knew where I was, but were they worrying about me? Probably. I wondered if my friends were worried, too. Had Mal or anyone talked to Mama and Daddy? (I didn't know that the Stoneybrook phones were out of order either.) I did know that Mary Anne and Mal were sitting at the Pikes' that night, and I wondered how they were doing, and whether Dawn and her mum had been able to pick up Jeff. What if they couldn't make the trip to the airport? Finally I worried about the parents of all the children who were stuck here.

"I didn't know you were such a worrier," said Quint as I poured out my thoughts to him. We were sharing my coat, sitting on it in a corner of one of the rehearsal rooms while excited children ran past by us.

"I'm not usually," I told him. "But this is an unusual situation. Aren't *you* worried? You haven't even talked to your parents yet."

"I know. But *I'm* safe, so I'm *not* worried. If my parents want to worry, that's their choice. There's nothing I can do about a blizzard. Or about talking to Mum and Dad. And as long as we're in this situation, we should make the best of it. This is quite fun, don't you think?"

"I don't know about fun, but it's an adventure. That's for sure." I glanced up then and saw Mme Noelle standing in the doorway, watching the rowdy children. I caught her eye. When she

158

nodded at me, I stood up. I pulled Quint with me. "I think Mme Noelle wants to speak to us," I said.

We dodged around children till we were facing my teacher. I'm usually shy with Madame, but maybe Quint's presence let me feel a little braver. At any rate, before Mme Noelle had started to speak, I said, "I think the children are ready to go to sleep—even if *they* don't realize it."

"I sink you are right," agreed Mme Noelle. She looked around uncertainly.

"Do you want me to help you settle them?" I asked. "I babysit all the time. I'm used to it."

"Me, too," said Quint. "I mean, I don't babysit, but I'm good at getting my brother and sister to go to sleep."

"Why, sank you, Jessica. Sank you, Queent," said Madame. "Zat would be a beeg help. Zee ozzer teachers and I would appreciate eet."

Maybe you're wondering where the older kids were. They were in another room, making the most of this night without their parents. They were eating and gossiping and doing each other's hair. I mean, the girls were. The boys were eating and gossiping and trying to repair this radio that has sat on a table in the office for about a hundred years—and never worked.

Quint and I divided the younger children into a group of boys and a group of girls. There were a lot more girls than boys, but that was okay. We

159

weren't making up teams or anything. Then Quint led the boys into one of the changing rooms and I led the girls to another. (A large bathroom leads off each changing room.) I helped the girls to wash their faces (with paper towels); to brush their teeth (with their fingers, using water); and to take off headbands, jewellery, and anything else that might be uncomfortable to sleep on. They packed these things in their dance bags and then returned to the practice room. Mme Duprès and Quint and I walked around while the children arranged their coats on the floor and lay down on them.

"Jessi?" called one of the very youngest girls. "This isn't comfy. I've got to sleep in my *bed*." Three minutes later she was so sound asleep that she didn't even wake up when the boys, who couldn't settle, accidentally kicked a trainer into the wall next to her during a game of Shoe Hockey (whatever that was).

Eventually, all the younger children managed to fall asleep. Quint and I crept out of the room and joined my friends.

"Hey, Jessi," said Katie Beth. "How about a nice cup of . . . soup?"

I groaned. Then I laughed. Katie Beth was teasing. It was only ten-thirty and already the "good" food (meaning the biscuits and the dried fruit) had long gone. Only the instant soup was left. Most of us were starving, but we couldn't face any more of those slimy noodles. Instead we just sat around and talked. Mme Noelle and the other teachers left us alone, which was considerate of them. (Or maybe just sensible. I'd heard Mme Duprès say she had a rip-roaring headache.) I talked to the girls; Quint talked to the boys. I would have liked to spend more time with Quint, but once I overheard him say "bowling bag" to this kid, Reed Creason, so I guessed they were talking about being male dancers, which was good for Quint. Anyway, Quint and I had the rest of the visit left for talking—provided his parents let him stay after the night's disaster which, by the way, I thought Quint had handled quite maturely.

The night passed quietly. Holly woke up once after a bad dream, but Mme Duprès helped her to go back to sleep. The older dancers and I slept in one of the other practice rooms, boys on one side, girls on the other—Mme Noelle in the middle.

I woke up at six o'clock with a stiff neck. (I wasn't used to sleeping on my coat, either). I rolled my head around, trying to loosen the tense muscles. Then I stood up and peered out of a window. Day was breaking. The snow was easing up and the sky was cloudy-bright.

By eight o'clock, everyone was up—and the phone was ringing non-stop. The storm was over. Parents would arrive as soon as the roads had been cleared. Quint waited in a queue to phone his parents. They had been worried, needless to say, but not much. They'd thought Quint (and I) were at my house in Stoneybrook. By the time they had realized just how bad the storm had become, the phones in Stoneybrook were already out of order, so they'd assumed Quint was safe but unreachable. (Which was the truth, in any case.)

When the phone calls died down, Mme Noelle announced "Zee coffee shop across zee street eez open, and Mr Wozneski, zee owner, has agreed to give us free breakfasts. Everybody, put on your coats!"

We ventured outside, Quint holding my hand. The snow ploughs hadn't come through Stamford yet, so we *waded* across the street. By the time we reached the coffee shop, most of us were soaked. But we didn't care. We were Mr Wozneski's only customers—and we took up nearly every booth. (Quint and I sat by ourselves at a small table.) After a night of instant soup, any food seemed wonderful, and Mr Wozneski fed us a feast while we dried out.

"This is rather romantic," I whispered to Quint, as we bit into bran-and-raisin muffins. (Dawn would have been proud of us.) "Snowbound at dance school, a cosy breakfast at a table for two."

"Yes," said Quint. "And this is only the beginning. We've still got two days together—and the dance tomorrow night."

162

"I *hope* the dance is still on," I said.

"If it isn't," replied Quint, "it won't matter. You and I will go to some other dance, some other time."

20th CHAPTER

Mary Anne

Thursday Morning

Here's what the Pike kids and I ate for breakfast on the day after the blizzard. Almost everything in the fridge and the cupboards. This may sound like a lot, but it wasn't. Not for nine hungry people. We ate a couple of apples and the ends of two loaves of bread. We ate a packet of instant oatmeal. We made tea without milk. Byron ate the last piece of cake. Adam ate a chicken T.V dinner....

We were scraping the bottom of the barrel. Everyone ate something that morning, but a lot of the food was strange (for breakfast), and Adam was the only one who left the table with a full stomach.

"Maybe," said Margo, "we could cook something new . . ."

"Like what?" I asked. (She was eyeing that box of icing mix.)

"Spaghetti with chocolate icing?" she suggested.

"Oh, sick!" said Adam.

"Just because you had a chicken dinner—" Nicky began to say.

"The freezer's full of vegetables," Mallory pointed out.

"I'd rather eat Margo's spaghetti," said Jordan.

"My tummy aches," said Claire.

"Uh-oh!" I replied.

"It's hungry. It's growling at me."

"Maybe Pizza Express is open now!" cried Mal.

"Oh, good idea." I'd almost got used to not having a phone. I realized I could order in food now. So I called Pizza Express. No answer. Then I called Chicken Wings (their ad: Speedy delivery, and service with a fryer). No answer. I called Tokyo House, even though it didn't open until noon, and even though Margo won't touch Oriental food. No answer. I called Chez Maurice, a fancy French restaurant that had probably never even heard of takeaway service. No answer.

After that I phoned Logan.

"I'm hungry," I whined before I'd said hello or good morning or anything civil. And before I'd asked him how he'd survived the storm.

"I'm sorry," Logan replied. "Where are you? At the Pikes'?"

"Yes. Mr and Mrs Pike got stuck in New York. They didn't come home last night. We're fine, though. Just hungry. There isn't much food left. Did anything interesting happen to you during the blizzard?"

"No," said Logan. "Well, except for when the power went out. Mum tried to phone the electricity board to tell them and then she found out the phone didn't work, either. She was really angry. But then she calmed down and she and Dad and Hunter and Kerry and I played Monopoly by the fireplace."

"Ooh, that sounds cosy," I said. "We didn't think of making a fire."

"We wouldn't have been allowed to make one," spoke up Mal from across the kitchen. "Not unless the heat had gone off, too."

"What?" said Logan.

"Mal was saying we wouldn't have been allowed to light a fire," I repeated. Then I said, "Guess what? Pizza Express isn't open."

"You're kidding!" exclaimed Logan. "The pizza place is closed at nine o'clock on a morning when we're snowed in and the snow ploughs haven't come through yet? What a shock!"

I laughed. "Okay, okay. Just remember you're speaking to a person who only had a tiny bowl of instant porridge for breakfast."

Byron nudged me. "Can I talk to Logan?" he asked.

"Of course." I handed him the phone.

"Now," said Byron, "you're speaking to a person who only had a tiny piece of sausage for breakfast."

I don't know what Logan replied, but whatever it was, it made Byron laugh and exclaim, "Oh, gross!" He gave the phone back to me.

"Mary Anne?" said Logan. "You know, I could—"

"Oh!" I cried, interrupting him. "I've just remembered something." I was looking out of the kitchen window at the back of Stacey's house.

"What's wrong?" asked Logan.

"Nothing. I mean, I don't know if anything's wrong. Last night we tried to phone the McGills and there wasn't any answer. This was after dinner, when the storm was really bad. And we couldn't see any lights at their house. But then the phones and everything went out. I should try to ring her now."

"You should ring Dawn, too," said Mal. "See if Jeff got in all right. And tell your dad we're okay."

I nodded. "Logan, we should ring off so that I can make some calls, okay?"

"Okay. See you later." And then he added softly, "Love you."

"'Bye," I said. I knew Logan would understand why I hadn't replied, "Love you, too." (The triplets wouldn't have let me hear the end of it.)

I dialled Stacey's number. No one answered. "That's really weird," I said to Mal. "Where could they be? Does it look as if they're at home?"

"I can't tell," Mal answered, peering out of the window. "Are you sure you dialled her number properly?"

I was pretty sure, but I dialled it again anyway. No answer.

"Phone Dawn," said Mal frowning.

My dad answered the phone. "At least *you're* home!" I exclaimed. "Can I talk to Dawn, please? Oh, and we're fine, Dad."

"Mary Anne, Dawn isn't here," said my father.

"Oh. Where is she?"

"Still at the airport. Jeff's plane was diverted to Washington because of the storm, and then the airport closed and Dawn and Sharon were stuck there overnight. I didn't hear from Sharon till a couple of hours ago."

"Oh, Dad!" I exclaimed. "You must have been scared to death." (And I was complaining because I hadn't eaten enough porridge that morning!)

"I was pretty nervous," my father agreed.

"But I'd heard on the transistor radio that the airport had been closed down, so I was hoping that's where they were. I certainly was relieved when the phone rang this morning."

"I expect you were," I said. I was going to tell Dad about Stacey, but before I could, our doorbell rang. "I'd better go," I said. "Someone's at the door, and half the Pikes aren't dressed yet. I'll ring you later. 'Bye!"

"Who's *that*?" yelled Vanessa, dashing upstairs in her nightdress.

"I don't know," I replied. "How could anyone have got over here? Nothing's been cleared yet. You'd need snowshoes to get around." I peeped out of the front window. "Or skis," I added.

You'll never guess in a million years who (what?) was standing in front of the Pikes' door.

Logan. On his cross-country skis. A rucksack was strapped to his back.

"I come bearing food," said Logan solemnly.

"I don't believe it!" I cried, laughing as Logan stepped inside.

"Hello, everybody!" he called. "I've brought food!"

"We're saved!" yelled Margo from her room.

A little while later, the Pike kids (dressed) and Logan and I were crowded around the kitchen table, which was piled high with bananas, peanut butter, bread, crackers, and carrot sticks.

"Real food," said Nicky, sighing with happiness.

"Logan," I said after a while, as the younger children drifted away from the table, "do you think we'll still have the dance tomorrow night?"

"The Winter Wonderland Dance," murmured Mal. "I'd almost forgotten about it. Gosh, I *hope* we have it."

"I wouldn't count on it," said Logan. "Not for tomorrow. That snow's really deep. Maybe the dance will be postponed till next week."

"It *can't* be postponed!" said Mal. "Ben and I can't wait till next week!"

"Mallory, can we go outside?" yelled Claire.

"Of course," Mal answered. "It's okay, isn't it, Mary Anne? This may be a once-in-a-lifetime experience. What with global warming and all."

The Pike children put on their layers of outdoor clothes. They spent the morning building a fancy sledging track in the back garden. Then they sailed along it on just about everything except a sledge—a saucer, a toboggan, a tray, their stomachs.

At one point, Logan skied over to Stacey's house. He rang the front doorbell. He knocked at their kitchen door. Then he skied back to me.

"No one came to the doors, and their car's gone," he reported.

"That's really weird," I said. "Do you think we should phone Claud?"

"What if Claud doesn't know where she is, either?" replied Mallory. "We'll just worry her.

Besides, Mrs McGill's gone too. I'm sure they're together, wherever they are. They probably just got stuck, like Dawn."

At that point I became convinced that Stacey and her mum had been in some horrible car accident during the storm. But since I've got a reputation as a big worrywart, I kept my mouth shut.

21st CHAPTER

Kristy

Thursday Morning

Honestly, sometimes I wish I were a boy. I know there aren't supposed to be big differences between boys and girls, but face it, how many boys do you know who pluck their eyebrows? Or put on make-up? Or curl their hair? Maybe they do if they're actors and they have to get ready for a play or something, but, for instance, I don't see Sam or Charlie doing those things before school every day. And those things take up a lot of time. To top it off, they're boring....

In case you haven't guessed, I didn't exactly appreciate having to get up at the crack of dawn *on a snowy day* in order to make myself look good, but that's what I did. I wasn't going to let Bart catch me with morning breath, sleepy eyes, and bed hair. So when my alarm went off, I tiptoed out of my room and down the hall to the bathroom.

I locked myself in.

Then I rummaged around in the cabinet under the basin.

I had decided that I might as well shave my legs for the first time.

Luckily for me, I found an electric razor *and* the power was back on. I stuck the plug into a socket. *Bzzzzz* went the razor. I ran it up and down my legs. When I'd finished, my legs didn't look all that different, though they certainly felt naked. What was the big deal?

I turned my attention to my face and hair. Against my better judgment I had a shower. The pipes in Watson's house (my house) are old and make a lot of noise. An early-morning shower on a snowy day wouldn't be appreciated. Oh, well. I didn't have any choice.

After my shower, I got out a hairdryer. It's Charlie's, believe it or not, but I didn't think he'd mind if I borrowed it. Then I found some old curling tongs I was about to use, when I decided I could probably electrocute myself since my hair was wet. So first I blew my hair dry and then I curled it. (My hair ended up looking and feeling like limp macaroni. A headband only made things worse.)

Well, on to make-up.

All I own is a leftover tube of mascara and some powder blusher. Even though I wanted to wear eye shadow and stuff, I thought the mascara and blusher would be tricky enough. Besides, Mum's got all the good make-up, and I couldn't very well sneak through her room and into her bathroom at 6 am. So I had to make do.

When I'd finished with the make-up, it looked great. It really did. And I'd been in the bathroom for an hour and a half.

I was no longer the only person up.

Bother! I hadn't counted on that. From my neck up I looked fantastic. Well, except for my macaroni hair. But below my neck I looked . . . I looked . . . like someone in her nightdress. With naked legs. And I didn't want Bart to see that. Frankly, I didn't want *any*one to see me, as I realised that I looked rather odd. But as I said, I wasn't the only one up.

I unlocked the bathroom door, planning to listen for a moment, hear nothing but silence, and make a dash for my room. Unfortunately, as soon as I unlocked the door I heard Sam say, "Gosh, Kristy! About time too!"

"What are you doing up?" I hissed.

"I want to enjoy every second of this day off school," he replied. "How long have you been in there? And what are you doing? You never act like such a girl. I didn't think I'd have to go through this until *Karen* was thirteen."

"By which time you'll be twenty-one and not living here any more, I hope."

"Very funny."

"Sam, just go back to your room for a sec, please," I said urgently.

"What about me?" said a second voice.

"David Michael?" I asked.

"Yeah. Kristy, I've got to *go*."

"Use your own bathroom," I said. (He and Karen and Andrew and Emily share a bathroom.)

"This one's closer."

"All right." I heaved an enormous sigh. Then I opened the door and strode into the hall. My brothers, each wearing a T-shirt and sweat pants, were leaning against the wall with their arms crossed. When Sam saw me, his eyes nearly popped out of his head. David Michael's mouth dropped open.

"Wrong holiday, Kristy," said Sam. "Christmas is coming, not Hallowe'en."

David Michael didn't say anything. He just ran into the bathroom, laughing.

I don't know who came to the conclusion that women gossip and men don't. My friends and I have learned that this is completely wrong.

Women and men both gossip. My brothers are prime examples of male gossips. By the time everyone was awake and at the breakfast table on Thursday morning, Sam and David Michael had spread the word about my appearance when I came out of the bathroom. Every head turned towards me as I slid into my place on the bench. (I noticed that Bart had been seated next to me.)

"'Morning, darling," said Mum.

"Nice hair," said Sam.

"Nice outfit," said Charlie. (Since I thought I *had* put together a rather nice outfit, I wasn't sure whether Charlie was being serious or sarcastic.)

"Nice make-up," said David Michael, and slapped his hand over his mouth, giggling.

"Hey, Watson, can we put a timer in our bathroom?" asked Sam. "There should be a sixty-minute limit on primping."

He turned to Andrew and asked, "Do you know what *primping* is, Andrew?" (Andrew frowned and shook his head.) "It's making yourself look beautiful."

"For your . . . *boyfriend*?" asked Andrew.

"Mum!" I cried.

"Sam!" cried Mum.

"Andrew!" cried Sam.

Andrew glanced around the table. "Emily!" he said finally, and everybody laughed. Even I laughed.

And during the laughter, when no one could

hear him, Bart whispered to me, "You look beautiful, Kristy."

I relaxed. "Thanks," I said.

Okay. I'd made it. Bart had spent the night at my house. He'd survived meals with my family. He put up with teasing by my brothers and sisters. And he hadn't gone away. Emotionally, I mean. He was sitting next to me, telling me I looked beautiful.

If Bart and I could weather that, we could weather anything.

I began to think about something other than myself. The storm, for instance. As soon as breakfast was over I took a good look out of the window. I found myself staring at an ocean of snow. It stretched from our front door, across the lawn, across the street, and across another lawn to Shannon Kilbourne's front door. It stretched up and down our road, smooth and rolling, snowdrifts making waves against houses and fences and trees.

Bart stood beside me. "This is the most snow I've ever seen," he said.

"I rather wish the snow ploughs wouldn't clear it," I replied. "They'll ruin the view."

"And, I won't have any excuse to stay here," added Bart. "I'll have to go home."

"Speaking of home," I said, "I wonder if Jeff arrived okay last night. I think I'll phone Dawn and Mary Anne." So I did. "Well for heaven's sake," I said to Bart when I'd rang off. "Guess what? Neither Mary Anne nor Dawn was there. Mary Anne's still at the Pikes' because Mr and Mrs Pike got stuck in New York. And Dawn's still at the airport! I didn't hear anything about people stranded at the airport on the news this morning. Just that the power's back on, the phones are working again, and what the current temperature is. I hope the newspaper's got better stories." Then it occurred to me to call the rest of my friends. Only Mallory was at home. She and Mary Anne were staying at her house until her parents got back.

"Call Stacey," Mal said. "No one's been able to reach her or her mum."

I dialled the McGills'. No answer.

So I called Claudia. Mr Kishi answered Claud's phone. "She's still at the Perkinses'," he told me. "They couldn't get home last night."

Wow! Pretty interesting. Before I called Claud at the Perkinses', I decided to phone Jessi. I wondered what sort of story she had.

"Jessi got stuck at dance school!" Becca told me excitedly. "Daddy couldn't pick her up. She ate breakfast at a *restaurant* this morning. Quint, too. He's with her. Mama and Daddy can't get them until the snow ploughs come."

I phoned Claud right away. "Have you got any idea what happened to the BSC last night?" I exclaimed. "Somebody should write about us.

Hey, where's Stacey? Mal's worried because Stace and her mum aren't back."

"They aren't back?" Claud repeated. "That's weird. Stacey rang me yesterday afternoon. She wanted me to come to the mall with her because she was getting her hair permed. I know she didn't have any plans last night. She and her mum were supposed to be at home. I wonder where they could be?"

I wondered, too.

And I began to worry.

22nd CHAPTER

Dawn

Wednesday Night
and Thursday Morning
I tried to sleep Wednesday
night. I really did. I read and
read and read. I was sure that
at some point I'd begin to nod
off. I don't know how Mum slept.
But she did. So did a lot of other
people. Not Carter, though. I met
Carter at about three in the
morning. At first, he scared me
to death . . . .

180

I think that if I'd been much younger I would have spent Wednesday night saying to my mother, "Now what time is it? . . . *Now* what time is it?" However, I was wearing a watch, so I just kept looking at it. I bet I checked it every two minutes. Nine thirty-three, nine thirty-five, nine thirty-seven, nine thirty-nine.

"Darling," said Mum after a while, "looking at your watch isn't going to make the time pass any more quickly."

I sighed. "I know. It's like drivers who think they can clear traffic jams by blasting their horns. The two things aren't connected."

Mum smiled at me. "Can't you concentrate on your book?"

"Not really. And the book's quite good. I just keep thinking about Jeff. I wonder if he knows why we aren't trying to phone him."

"He probably does," my mother replied. "When nobody in Washington can reach anyone here, they'll work it out. Also, maybe Jeff has spoken to Richard. I'm sure Jeff will have tried to ring home."

"Oh, yes," I said, brightening. "Of course."

"Feel better?"

"Yup."

"Ready to sleep?"

"Nope. But maybe I can read now."

"Okay. Listen, I'm sure the airport's safe, but don't go wandering around during the night without me. Let me know if you want to go to the toilet or the snack bar. I'll come with you."

Ordinarily, I might have thought Mum was being unreasonably overprotective, but not that night. I glanced at the empty corridors, at the frustrated and tired people around me, and I shivered.

"No problem," I said to Mum. "Um, are you going to sleep now?"

"I might have a little nap," she answered.

"Let's go to the toilet first."

So we did. When we got back to our seats, Mum didn't just have a nap, she fell into a deep sleep.

I sat up with my book. I tried different positions. I flung my legs over the armrest. The armrest hurt the backs of my knees. I curled into a ball, but couldn't find a good place for my head. I tried Mum's position, sitting up straight. She looked as if she was at a smart restaurant, waiting to be served dinner. But her eyes were closed. Also, she was snoring.

I hoped no one would hear. Or if they did hear, that they wouldn't realize the sounds were coming from my mother. Then I hoped they wouldn't think *I* was snoring. I made a big show of looking awake.

At midnight I asked the woman behind the desk when she thought Jeff's plane would arrive.

"Around seven, maybe," she replied.

At two o'clock, she went off duty. A man took

her place. I asked *him* when Jeff's plane would arrive.

"Probably beforc midday," he answered. (Some help!)

I went back to my seat. I snuggled against my coat. I closed my eyes. Then I opened them. I looked at the other people trying to sleep. Opposite me was an older couple. In another row was a family—mum, dad, and three little boys. A lot of people seemed to be travelling by themselves.

My eyes started to droop. In all honesty, I don't think I fell asleep, though. *Maybe* I did, but I doubt it. Anyway, a little while later I was lolling in the chair, my eyes closed, remembering what Mum had said earlier about the airport and whether it was safe, when I became convinced that someone was standing silently behind me, staring. I was trying to decide whether turning round and opening my eyes would be foolish, when I felt a hand on mine.

I nearly shrieked.

I knew it wasn't Mum's hand. She hadn't stirred.

"Ah-ma-*mah*!" crowed a little voice. A baby's?

Sure enough, when I found the courage to turn round, I was looking into a pair of deep black eyes, which gazed seriously at me from a brown face. After a moment, the cheeks dimpled into a smile.

"Hello, there," I whispered. "Where did you

183

come from?" Then I recognized the boy as one of the children in the family I'd noticed earlier. I sat up and looked for them. There were his brothers and his mother, sound asleep. But where was his father?

"Carter!" called a panicky voice.

There was the father. He was running along the corridor, carrying a nappy bag. I got to my feet and picked up the baby. "Is this who you're looking for?" I asked the man.

"Carter! Thank heavens!" he said, reaching for the baby. "Where did you find him?" he asked me.

"Right here. I just opened my eyes and there he was."

The man shook his head, smiling. "Carter's our little night owl," he said. "He just won't sleep. He wants to stay up and play. I decided to walk him to the cloakroom so that I could change him, and . . . I don't know. How can such short legs move so quickly? I wish he would drop off for a while."

Carter's dad and I chatted till Carter actually did drop off. By then, even I was feeling drowsy, and finally I managed to doze, my head resting on Mum's shoulder. The doze turned into sleep.

The next thing I knew, it was nearly seven-thirty. I opened my eyes to a bustling airport (bustling compared with the middle of the night) and a glaringly white world.

"Good morning, sleepyhead!" teased my mother.

"Sleepyhead! I didn't fall asleep till about four. I feel as if I've been to a sleep-over—on a school night. When's Jeff going to be here? Is he already on his way? Hey, I'm hungry!"

"Let's eat breakfast, then," said Mum, "and I'll tell you what's been happening." She stood up, closing her book.

"I must look awful," I said, yawning. "Just what I always wanted. To wake up with fifty other people."

"Well, nobody here is a raving beauty," said Mum. "Not at this hour after a night in a waiting room."

Mum and I went to the snack bar for breakfast. I told her about Carter, and she gave me a blizzard/airport update: The storm was over. Seventy centimetres of snow had fallen at the airport. The airport was in the process of re-opening. Jeff was due to arrive around 11:15. The phones worked. Mum had spoken to Richard. Richard had *not* spoken to Jeff, since both the electricity and the phones had been off in Stoney-brook the night before. Mum had tried to call Jeff in Washington that morning and hadn't been able to reach him (he was travelling, with his personal flight attendant, from the hotel to the airport), but she had spoken to another flight attendant, who said that Jeff *was* upset, but at least he was all in one piece.

After breakfast, Mum and I waited. I went to the cloakroom and tried to wash and make myself look presentable. I watched snow ploughs clear the runways. I played with Carter and his brothers.

At 11:15 Mum and I were among a crowd of people pressed against the windows, watching the arrival of the plane that should have arrived about fifteen hours earlier. Everyone cheered as the plane touched down. Then we moved to the gate, to greet the passengers as they left the plane. Jeff (with his flight attendant) was one of the first people to come into the terminal. When he and Mum and I spotted each other, all three of us burst into tears.

Jeff hugged Mum and wouldn't let go of her.

"I thought I'd never get here," he said. "I thought I'd never see you."

"We were worried," Mum replied, sniffling. "We tried to phone, but we couldn't reach you. Everyone kept saying you were all right, though. The phones stopped working. We couldn't ring you or Richard or anyone."

"Mum and I spent the night here!" I announced.

"Really?" said Jeff. "You waited for me all this time?"

"Of course!" exclaimed Mum. Then she added,

"What an adventure you've had! Was the hotel nice?"

Jeff perked up. "I used room service!" he exclaimed, as Mum and I put on our coats and the three of us made our way towards the luggage carousel. "They said I could order whatever I wanted for breakfast. So I had sausages and chips and toast."

"Very well-balanced," I commented.

The more Jeff talked, the happier he sounded. He even sounded *proud*. After we had found his suitcase and we were walking towards the car, he said, "You know, I wasn't the only kid travelling alone. There was this little girl. She was only eight." (Jeff's only ten.) "And she just kept crying. She thought we'd been hijacked! And while we were circling round and round she was airsick. Do you know what was in my hotel room?" Jeff went on.

"What?" said Mum and I. We had found our car and were unlocking it and loading in Jeff's suitcase.

"A shoehorn. And I was allowed to *keep* it. It's in my suitcase. I'm going to give it to Richard for Christmas. In his stocking."

Jeff chattered all the way to Stoneybrook. As we turned onto our street, he exclaimed, "You know, last night wasn't so bad after all!"

A few minutes later, we had a happy reunion

with Richard. Then he said, "Dawn, Mary Anne wants you to phone her. She's at the Pikes'."

I dialled Mal's number, and Mary Anne answered the phone. "Dawn! I'm so glad you're back!" she cried. "But guess what? Stacey and her mother are missing!"

23rd
CHAPTER

Stacey

Wednesday Evening
and Thursday Morning
Doo-dee, doo-doo, doo-dee, doo-
doo. I was in a scene from a
<u>Twilight Zone</u> show. My mom and I
were lost on a lonely dark road at
nighttime during a snowstorm, and
suddenly...

The man was looming in the window of our car. (Actually, he seemed quite concerned, but I didn't think about that till later.) And Mum was looking at me, waiting for me to say, "Why, I think climbing into a car with a strange man is a wonderful idea!"

We *were* in a pretty tight spot, though. I mean, even without the man. We really didn't know where we were, we were stuck in a car without heat in the middle of a raging blizzard, and I was famished. I suppose you have to take a chance and trust people sometimes. Anyway, I was with Mum.

I nodded my head. "Okay," I whispered.

Mum turned to the man. "Thank you," she said. "We'd love to go home with you. I don't know what would have happened if you hadn't come along. You must be a miracle."

The man grinned. "I'm Ken Schiavone," he said as Mum and I climbed out of our car. (We locked the doors and just left the car sitting by the side of the road, half buried in snow.)

"I'm Maureen McGill," said Mum, "and this is my daughter, Stacey. We live in Stoneybrook. We were on our way home from the Washington Shopping City."

Mr Schiavone held his car doors open for Mum and me and we slid in, Mum in the front, me in the back.

"I wasn't sure I was going to get home myself,"

said Mr Schiavone, as he urged his car forward. "I haven't seen weather like this for years."

"Where did you say you live?" I asked. "At the end of the road?"

"Not quite the end," Mr Schiavone replied. "But further down the road. My wife and I moved in last year. We bought a Victorian monstrosity. Six months ago we had our first baby," he added proudly. "Mason. He's something of a monstrosity himself."

"You've got a baby?" I repeated.

Mum turned round and smiled at me. Then she said to Mr Schiavone, "Stacey loves children. She's a wonderful babysitter."

"That's terrific. I'm sure Mason will be glad to see a new face." Mr Schiavone nosed the car into a dark turning. I couldn't see anything. No house, no lights. I could barely make out the drive we were travelling along.

This is it, I thought. He's taking us deep into the woods, and Mum and I will never be seen alive again. We'll finish up as a story in one of those books about missing people and strange disappearances.

I was working myself into a pretty good panic when suddenly a beautiful house appeared through the snow, as if by magic. It looked like a house from a fairy tale, lit inside and out, a green wreath with a tartan ribbon hanging on the door,

191

the gold lights on a Christmas tree twinkling through a window.

"Ooh!" I said, as Mr Schiavone pulled into the garage. "This is beautiful."

"Thank you. I must confess, my wife and I love Christmas. We put up decorations about a week ago. We like to enjoy a long Christmas."

"That's nice," said Mum. "Stace, maybe you and I should have an old-fashioned Christmas this year."

"Maybe," I replied. This Christmas would be my first as a divorced kid, and I wasn't sure how I felt about the holiday.

Mum and I followed Mr Schiavone into his house, through the kitchen, and to the living room, another fairy-tale sight. There was the tree I had seen from outside. Stacks of presents were already piled under it. A fire was blazing in the fireplace, and on the chimney above had been hung another wreath, similar to the one on the door, but twice its size. And sitting in an armchair was Mrs Schiavone, who was reading a story to Mason. What was she reading? *The Night Before Christmas*, of course.

Mrs Schiavone looked up in surprise when Mum and I trailed into the living room after Mr Schiavone.

"Hi, darling. I've brought along a couple of visitors for the night. They were stranded a little way down the road," said Mr Schiavone.

"Our car broke down," Mum added apologetically. "We were stranded."

Mrs Schiavone stood up, shifting Mason to her hip. "My goodness!" she said. "Here. Take off your wet things. Dry out by the fireplace. I'll add two plates to the table. . . . Where do you live?"

The adults introduced themselves again, and Mum told Mrs Schiavone our story. "I suppose there's no point in phoning the AA," she said. "Not at this hour, in this weather."

"Of course not," agreed Mrs Schiavone. "Please. Spend the night here. You can phone the AA first thing in the morning. Is there anyone you need to phone now? Your husband?"

"No, no," said Mum quickly. "We're divorced. It's just Stacey and me. I don't think we need to make any phone calls. But . . ."

"Yes?" prompted Mrs Schiavone.

"Stacey's diabetic."

"No sugar for me," I interrupted, "and I need to give myself some insulin."

Mrs Schiavone was great. She showed me to the bathroom. As soon as I came out, she handed Mason to me and hurried into the kitchen, followed by Mum, saying, "Just tell me what Stacey can eat. We've got plenty of food here."

I sat by the fire, holding Mason and becoming very aware of the smell of my new perm. Mason noticed it, too, I think. He kept wrinkling up his nose. But when I picked up *The Night Before*

Christmas and began to read to him again, he settled down. "Do you like stories, Mason?" I asked.

"He loves to be read to," said Mr Schiavone from across the room. "We've been reading to him since the day he came home from the hospital."

Hmm. Good information. I stored it away, planning to mention it at the next BSC meeting. *Even little babies like to be read to.*

Considering that the evening had started out to be so frightening, it ended really nicely. The Schiavones and Mum and I had a great time together. Mr and Mrs Schiavone were . . . wonderful. Funny, warm, matter-of-fact (my diabetes didn't upset them a bit; they just asked what I could eat and then arranged it for me), understanding (no more questions about Dad or the divorce), interesting, outgoing, involved, creative—you name it. And Mason was charming. The Schiavones let me put him to bed. I wished they lived closer to Stoneybrook so that we could be friends and I could babysit for Mason.

By the next day, Mum and I almost didn't want to leave, and the Schiavones seemed reluctant to say goodbye. So we hung around together, putting off calling the AA, using the snow as an excuse. And it *was* a pretty good excuse. Mr Schiavone leaned out of the front door on Thursday morning and stuck a metre rule into the snow.

All but thirty centimetres were covered. Seventy centimetres of snow had fallen.

"Remember this," Mum told me. "You may not see the likes of it again."

The morning passed, the sun came out, and eventually the snow ploughs cleared even the minor country roads. Mum had no more reasons for not calling the AA. By one o'clock, we were on our way home.

We took the motorway.

I insisted.

"The snow's awfully pretty, isn't it?" said Mum.

"Now that the sun's shining, the road's been cleared, the car works, and we know where we're going," I answered.

Mum laughed. She drove home slowly. It was nearly two o'clock when we finally reached our house. To my surprise, I saw Claudia standing in our front porch. When we pulled up in the street (our drive wasn't cleared, of course), she bolted across the snowy garden and threw her arms round me as I climbed out of the car.

"Oh, my lord!" she cried. "You're safe! You're alive!"

Now, how did Claud know that a stranger had picked us up and taken us to his house deep in the woods?

"Where *were* you?" exclaimed Claudia. "Have

195

you really been gone since yesterday? You scared us to death!''

I looked at Mum, then back to Claud. "I didn't think anyone would even realize we weren't at home," I said.

"We weren't sure till this morning," Claud told me. "Yesterday Mal and Mary Anne couldn't see any lights on in your house, and they couldn't get you on the phone. But then the power went off and the phones went off so we couldn't tell whether you'd come home later or not. But when we couldn't reach you today we panicked."

"I'm sorry," I said, as Claud walked Mum and me to the front door. "But what's wrong? Why were you trying to get hold of us?"

"We just wanted to know if you were all right. You wouldn't believe what happened to everyone last night! Jessi got stuck in Stamford and spent the night at her dance school; the Perkinses couldn't come home, so I spent the night with Myriah and Gabbie and Laura; Dawn and her mum spent the night at the airport . . ."

Claudia went on and on. She listened to my story. Then she said, "I'd better ring Kristy. She'll want to know this." So she rang her, and a few moments later she was saying, "What? You're kidding?! I'll spread the word!" When she rang off she said to me, "School will be open tomorrow, and the dance is still on. Kristy just talked to that kid she knows—the one whose mother is on the school board. We were afraid the dance would be called off because of the snow."

Claud phoned the other BSC members, and before I knew it, the entire club had gathered at my house. Logan and Quint, too.

"Don't ever think we wouldn't miss you," Claud said to me.

"Yes, I'm very nosy," added Mal. "I can usually tell whether you're at home or not, and it matters to me."

"Okay, okay. I'll keep in touch!" I said. "That's a promise."

Then we went outside. We built a mammoth snowman and snow woman in our front garden.

"Look. They're ready for the Winter Wonderland Dance," whispered Mary Anne. "Just like we are."

"Tomorrow night's going to be magic," I said.

"But most important,"added Kristy,"the BSC will be there *together*."

EPILOGUE

Kristy

"OH! oh, my—Mum! Hey, Mum!"

"Kristy, what on earth is going on?" asked my mother.

"Mum, you'll never guess who was on the phone! That was Marian Tan, the woman from the *Stoneybrook News*. I mean, the editor. And she wants to print my article. Honestly. She really likes the idea. And she's going to *pay* me!"

"That's fantastic, darling," said Mum.

"Gosh, I'll have to get cracking."

"Haven't your friends already written about their blizzard experiences?" Mum wanted to know.

"Yes, but there's too much material for one newspaper article. I've got to trim it down. And make it fit together. Besides, we're all still working on our final entries—you know, how things ended up, what happened after the storm, how the Winter Wonderland Dance went. That kind of thing."

I was pretty sure that a phone call saying "SNOWBOUND!" was going to be published would bring in those last pieces of material quickly. And I was right. By the next day, I had everything I needed for the article:

You aren't really going to publish this stuff, are you, Kristy? The stuff about Logan and me and the dance? What does that have to do with the blizzard? Well, I suppose it is sort of connected. Anyway, so Logan stayed at the Pikes' with Mal and me until Mr and Mrs Pike returned from New York. His food came in very handy, since we ate it for lunch, too. I'm not quite so glad he skied over, though. In the afternoon, Adam tried to use the skis and nearly killed himself.

The dance on Friday was wonderful. It was dreamy.

199

Kristy

Kristy, you don't want all the details, do you? They're private. Logan and I had fun, that's all.

                    Mary Anne

Jeff seems to be over his ordeal. I think Mum and I are, too. The three of us took lo-o-o-o-ng naps when we got home from the airport. Somehow, the plows cleared almost all the roads in Stoneybrook by Thursday night. So school was open on Friday. And the dance was held. Price Irving and I went as planned. You know something? Remember how I had that enormous crush on Price? Well, I nearly forgot about him (and the dance) when I was so concerned about Jeff. Maybe Price isn't as important to me as I had thought. Who knows? Anyway, we had a good time.

                    Dawn

Maria and Gabbie had so much fun
playing outdoors on Thursday. They
bilt the snow family they had talked
about and they made snowballs and
snow angles and pulled each other
around on the sled. Rigth before lunch-
time, Jamie Newton and some other kids
came over to play. I had to stay
inside with Laura, but I kept an eye on
the kids though the kichen window

Mr and Mrs Perkins came home not
long after Jamie came over. You shold
have see the greeting Mariah and Gabby
gave their parnets. It was grate. They
hugged them and huged them.

Iri and I had a grate time at the
dance I think mabe I like him beter
than just a freind!

Claudia

Heaven. I'm in heaven.
The dance was
wonderful. Quint is
wonderful. Life is
wonderful.

Jessi

Kristy

Mum and Dad got home in the nick of time. Mary Anne and I had reached the end of our rope. We were tired of crackers, tired of complaints, and tired of hearing about the Abominable Snowman. We were even tired of snow itself. If the storm had canceled the dance, I would have... Well, I'm not sure what I would have done, but it would have been drastic. Luckily, the dance was held after all. I am not the world's best dancer, but Ben doesn't care, which is one reason I like him. Now I can't wait for the Valentine's Day Dance.

Mallory

I'm still sorry for giving you lot such a scare.

It's funny, but some good things came from the awful experience Mum and I had. One, we got to know the Schiavones. As soon as we came home, Mum mailed a Christmas card to them, and today we got one back, with a picture of Mason. Mum is going to invite the Schiavones to dinner some time in January.

Two, Mum and I are closer. She was impressed to see that I really do keep my insulin injection kit with me at all times. And in a backward sort of way, I was almost relieved to see Mum get scared on Wednesday night. It is nice to know that parents are not perfect.

Three, even though we made you all worry, it was quite nice for Mum and me to realize just how much you care about us.

Let me see. The dance was okay, but someone should tell Austin that since he does not yet shave, he should not wear after-shave lotion. By the way, my perm looked fantastic, but I'm not sure it was worth getting stranded in a snowstorm.

Stacey

The dance was awesome. Bart and I had so much fun. We didn't actually dance very much, but we hung around with Mary Anne and Logan and Jessi and Quint and everyone. Bart showed the boys how to turn their eyelids inside out. Somehow, this did not seem immature. Just fun.

I applied my own make-up before the dance, and Bart told me (again) that I looked beautiful.

Kristy

I hope I did. This time, I spent nearly two hours preening in the bathroom. Also, I bought Bart a blue carnation and he bought me an orchid corsage!

I guess I better go. I have to call Bart. He's going to come over and help me write the newspaper article.

Kristy

Oh, Karen wants to add something here:

EMILY JUNIOR IS BACK. SILLY OLD DAVID MICHAEL RATNAPPED HER.

AND WE ALL LIVED HAPPILY EVER AFTER.

THE END